RACING

KYLIE GILMORE

Racing: © 2022 by Kylie Gilmore

Cover design by: Michele Catalano Creative

Published by: Extra Fancy Books

ISBN-13: 978-1-64658-037-8

What if your one-night stand is your one true love?

1

Eve

I'm about to be an aunt! My older sister, Jenna, is in labor right this minute. If only teleportation devices were real, then I'd port from LA to Summerdale in a nanosecond! I wish. The soonest I could get a flight out to New York is tomorrow afternoon. By then the baby should be here. We don't know if it's a boy or a girl. She wanted to be surprised.

I park my silver Prius near the baby store Stork Rave. I've passed this shop hundreds of times. Not once have I ever had a reason to go in. I have zero experience with babies. All of my friends are single or married without kids.

I'm jittery with energy as I walk down the sidewalk, thinking of Jenna in labor, all that pain and the waiting. She told me first babies usually take the longest to come out. She's been in labor for an hour now at the hospital and hours before that at home. I've been hyperfocused ever since she called to let me know this was the real deal. I've booked my flight, packed, emailed my boss that it's finally time for that week off he promised me, and now I'm at the baby store for a welcome-baby present.

I pull open the door to Stork Rave, instantly overwhelmed with everything baby. The place is bigger than I realized from the storefront, going far back, with row after row of baby gear. There's a lower level too. Lotta pregnant women in here with their doting husbands looking at cribs, changing tables, clothes, and diaper thingies. What *is* that thing? It looks like a space-age trash can. Do you need a special trash can for diapers?

Feeling conspicuous in my belted shirt dress with no bulge to speak of, I wander to the clothing section on my right. Wow. Huge gender divide here. The girl side is dominated by way too much pink. Jenna wouldn't like that, would she? I actually don't know. She's my older sister, but I've only recently gotten to know her again. We reunited two years ago after not having seen each other since we were young kids, the fallout of our parents' messy divorce. The judge asked us in court to decide whom we wanted to live with. Jenna chose Mom; I chose Dad. I resisted visiting Mom and Jenna as a kid, feeling like I'd chosen a side, and Jenna had chosen against me. I was nine.

Jenna and I had a lot of catching up to do as adults, which hasn't been easy living on opposite sides of the country. We've kept in touch with weekly phone calls and daily texts, along with a few visits back and forth. I'm happy to say I feel close to her again, even though I don't know her personal tastes for her baby's wardrobe.

"Can I help you?" a cheerful saleswoman asks. She takes a surreptitious look at my flat belly and smiles blandly at me. "Is the mom registered here?"

"No. I'm just looking, thanks." I casually step to the next section and find myself surrounded by industrial-looking bras, breast pads, creams, and giant suction things. Ah, breast pumps. That looks painful.

I just don't know what to get for a new baby. I head downstairs, which is full of more gear—car seats, strollers, and playpens. Obviously, I need something I can fit into my luggage.

Oh! There's a cute little fluffball! A gray stuffed animal sits against the far wall. Someone must've changed their mind about buying it, or maybe it fell off a nearby shelf. I should get something like that for Jenna's baby.

I step closer. "Ah!" I slap a hand over my mouth. It moved!

My eyes are glued to the thing as I creep closer. "Any store employees around?" I call out. "There's something furry and alive in here." What if it's a rat? Someone should definitely get that thing out of here. But then I hear a sound, a teeny cry like a baby.

I walk over and peer down. It's a tiny gray kitten. *Aww.* It looks up at me with green eyes and lets out its baby cry again. Not quite a meow, it's high-pitched like it's calling for its mama.

I scoop it up, and it climbs to my shoulder, kneading me through the cotton fabric of my dress. *Ouch.* I hold it up, gently removing its claws from the fabric. "How did you get in here?"

"I didn't know they offered kittens for adoption here," a deep voice says. "Seems like my work follows me."

I turn and meet the sparkling sky-blue eyes of a gorgeous man. My breath catches in my throat. He's probably early thirties, taller than me, which is always nice for a woman of five feet ten. Tiny laugh lines feather out of the corners of his eyes. I've seen my fair share of good-looking men in LA, mostly actors, but this man has something different about him. A warmth in his gaze. His blue eyes stand out in contrast to his short dark hair and olive skin. High cheekbones, a square jaw with a hint of stubble. He *must* be a model. He's dressed casually in a white T-shirt that emphasizes his broad shoulders and the curves of his biceps. His faded jeans fit perfectly to his long legs.

I'm barely aware of kitten claws kneading my shoulder again. A flush creeps up my neck as the man closes the distance between us. My breathing accelerates, my heart pumping hard. It's like I went for a run without all the messy sweat.

He flashes a charming smile, his teeth flashing white

against his skin. "Is this the new trend in LA? Shopping with your cat?"

I blink a few times, breathless. "I just found her." My voice sounds high-pitched, and I work to bring it back to normal. "I don't know where she came from."

"May I?" he asks, gesturing toward the kitten. "I'm a veterinarian."

I take a steadying breath and hand her over. Not a model. Maybe I should get a cat just to visit this veterinarian. Too bad my apartment building doesn't allow pets. I want to fan myself, but manage to keep my hands at my sides.

He inspects her underbelly and checks her teeth before gently stroking the kitten's head. "It's a boy. Probably nine weeks old. It's possible he wandered in from the alley, where his mother and the rest of his litter are nearby, or from someone's house. He doesn't look malnourished, so I suspect someone is looking after him."

That deep voice does something to me, scraping against my insides. I could listen to him recite the dictionary. I'm not usually like a teenager faced with her longtime crush. I've been told I come off as cool, as in icy. I suspect that has more to do with my blond hair, pale blue eyes, and reserved nature than with my true nature. Passion and drama burn through me directly onto the pages of my scripts. I'm a TV writer for an awesome one-hour dramedy show, *Irreverent*, about a multigenerational family. I also have several fantastic feature-film scripts sitting unsold on my laptop.

He hands the kitten back to me, his long fingers grazing the side of my hand, sending an electric shiver up my arm. I pet the little gray kitten along one cheek, trying to ignore the sensations rioting through me. "Did you get lost?"

The kitten purrs, his tiny body vibrating as he leans his head against my hand.

"You've got the magic touch," the gorgeous veterinarian says.

My mind races. It's rare I'm this attracted to a guy right away. Should I ask him out for a drink or something? I wonder if he's from around here. The truth is, part of me longs for someone to share my life with, and part of me is afraid to move forward with a serious relationship. I'm stuck, which is an extremely frustrating place to be. I blame Jenna. Her marriage is a strong, happy one, and it made me realize that if she can have that, after having gone through the same trauma from our parents' divorce as I did, maybe it could happen for me too.

So what did I do after this major realization? Freaked out and deleted the dating app from my phone. If I could skip straight to what Jenna and Eli have, that would be one thing. But the whole bumpy journey to find that one rare match scares me. All I've known are mismatched people, arguments that turn into someone leaving, and abandonment. Not for me. I think. I've been so conflicted for the last six months because of this longing deep inside.

Do I really want a man in my life, or do I just want good sex once in a while? It's been a long time since I've had either.

See, I have a history of poor choices in relationships from my early twenties, including a failed marriage—a combo of my low self-esteem and addiction to painkillers following knee surgery. I'm clean now at twenty-nine with only the occasional drink and no drugs ever. Years of therapy have gotten me to a place where I have higher standards for whom I'll be with.

Come on, Eve. You never meet a guy like this just going about your day. Between my long hours working in a TV writers' room and writing yet another feature-length screenplay in my spare time, the only people I've seen are my coworkers. Eight men, three women. The guys are like brothers to me at this point. I know what their burps smell like.

Gah! I know I need to push myself to be open to meeting new people if I'm ever going to get unstuck. And today I met someone, no app required. *Say something!*

He's so close I can see the thin dark blue line bordering his sky-blue eyes framed by thick dark lashes. His clean scent washes over me, fresh soap and something familiar, like the ocean. Maybe his cologne. It's delicious.

He rubs the kitten under the jaw with one finger, and the kitten preens under his touch, closing his eyes in bliss. "I'm Dominic."

My breath hitches. "Eve." I'm strangely tempted to reach up and feel the scruff of his jaw.

"Oh, Frankie!" a store employee says, rushing toward us. Her name badge says Connie. "Sorry! I had him in the back with me while I was having lunch, and he must've escaped. Where'd you find him?"

I hand the kitten over. "He was just hanging out by the back of the store."

She cuddles him close. "I couldn't bear to be separated from him all day. My boss said it was okay. I just got him last week."

"Mystery solved," Dominic says.

My gaze locks with his, a question hanging in the air between us. Is this the end or the beginning? My mouth is dry, my stomach light, like when I drive too fast over a speed bump. A moment of weightlessness, a rush of excitement.

"I should—" he starts.

I cut him off, realizing he wants to leave, and this is "end scene," as we say in the biz. "I'll be heading up." I point to the upper level. Sometimes my imagination gets the best of me, thinking this was the start of something. My life is filled with ordinary moments I embellish to make them extraordinary. I bet if I asked my best friend her opinion of Dominic, she wouldn't think he was as gorgeous as a model. She'd probably say he reminded her of the guy next door. All in my imagination, enhanced by my six-month dry spell.

He gives me a small smile, the laugh lines crinkling at the corners of those sparkling blue eyes. My stomach flutters. He really *is* that gorgeous. I turn and swiftly make my way to the stairs, a little deflated. It's not often I meet such a beautiful man. And a veterinarian. He loves animals, so that translates to a good guy with a gentle touch. Maybe I should've asked him out. Though it's entirely possible he was solely interested in the welfare of a stray kitten and not me.

Once I get to the upper level, I find the stuffed-animal section and pick up a cute giraffe. Nice and gender neutral. It could be a boy or girl giraffe—we'll never know—with a nice long neck for the baby to hang onto. I assume that's what a baby would do with a stuffed giraffe. Either that or chew it.

I take the giraffe to the cash register. The person in front of me leaves, and I step forward. "Hi."

The cashier, a perky redhead, smiles brightly. Her name tag says Melody. "Hello, would you like a gift bag?"

"That would be great." I reach into my purse for my wallet, but it's not there. *Shit.* I just packed my smaller travel purse to be sure I could fit everything, and I'd thought I'd shifted the essentials back to this purse for my shopping trip. How could I have forgotten my wallet? It dawns on me that I switched to a smaller wallet to fit in the smaller travel purse. The larger wallet, sitting on my kitchen table, only has a handful of nonessential rewards cards. I try to travel light, so I don't have to check anything and deal with baggage claim. I'm only away for a week. That was the most time I could get off work, and I was lucky to get it. We're in the middle of the season.

I search my large purse for stray cash and come up with two dollars and fifty-three cents. Not going to cut it. I pull my phone out. I never added a credit card to my phone app. Maybe I could use my bank app for my debit card? I click on the bank app, and it prompts me for my password. I never store passwords on my phone because my friend told me it's better not to because of hackers. I don't know if that's true, but I wish I hadn't listened to him because I can't remember the password. This is embarrassing.

Melody the cashier hands me a tall gift bag. The giraffe's head pokes out of the top.

I give her a weak smile. "I'm so sorry. I seem to have forgotten my wallet. Can you hold that for me? I have to drive home to get it. I'll be back in an hour."

"I've got it," a deep voice says behind me. Goosebumps break out on my arms.

I turn to face Dominic. "You really don't have to do that."

"Hey, I'm here for all animals, even the stuffed kind. Besides, I got the same thing." He puts his stuffed giraffe on the counter, along with a blue paisley pouch that, according to the picture, the mom is supposed to stuff the baby in like a kangaroo. I've seen front carriers and backpacks for babies but not pouches.

It suddenly occurs to me that the guy I'm lusting over is buying these things for *his wife and kid*. My lust instantly cools. I'd never mess around with a married man. Those vows should be sacred. Too many people get hurt if they're taken lightly. He's not wearing a wedding ring, but that doesn't always mean a guy is single.

"That's okay," I say. "I'm heading home to get my wallet. I'll be back."

I walk out, feeling a little light-headed. It's just the relief of getting out of a store where I clearly don't belong. I tell myself I'm in a good place in my life with my dream job—this year I was promoted to story editor—and I have a nice North Hollywood apartment with no roommates to contend with. What's not to love?

I get to the end of the block and stop, realizing I'm walking in the wrong direction. That store got me all discombobulated.

I do an about-face and head toward my car just as Dominic steps out of the store, holding two gift bags with giraffe heads sticking out of them.

"Glad you're still here," he says. "Your giraffe awaits. Let me guess, it's for a baby shower, and you don't know the sex, so you went with a gender-neutral item."

I cross to him. "Did you notice how the clothes are so gender-specific?"

"Hard to miss."

His delicious scent has me nearly light-headed again.

Chill. He's probably married. "My sister's in labor right this minute. It's a welcome-baby present."

He hands me the gift bag. "Mine is for a friend whose wife just had a baby."

My heart picks up a rapid beat, a sliver of hope slipping through. "You look like the married type. I would've guessed it was for your wife."

"I do?" He pauses, searching my expression, his eyes sharp with intelligence. "Are you trying to find out if I'm single?"

Busted! A rare blush creeps up my neck. I play it casual. "Sure."

"Yes. You?"

"Yes."

He holds my gaze for a long moment. "Well, it was *really* nice meeting you. Unfortunately, I'm flying home tomorrow. I'm here for a veterinary conference and extended my stay to visit my friend; otherwise, I'd ask you out for a drink of the hot or cold variety. Green smoothies seem to be all the rage here."

My lips curve up, hope blossoming. Dominic could help me answer the question I've been wrestling with—am I just missing sex or a man in my life? No one will get hurt because we both know going in that it's just for one night.

He smiles back, a warm smile that feels like sunshine all over my body. "I really like the way you look at me."

This time I give in to temptation, lifting a hand and stroking the scruff of his jaw. I look up into smoldering blue eyes.

He tips my face up to his, so close his breath fans over my lips. "Are you happy that I'm here for one night, or that I wanted to take you out for a drink?"

"Yes."

He flashes a smile before dipping his head, his lips grazing my temple. He meets my eyes, checking in with me, a smile playing over his lips before he leans close again, brushing a kiss over my cheek and jaw.

I shift toward him just as he pulls away, my lips meeting his, a jolt going through me on contact. He takes over, cradling my jaw in one large hand, his kisses a gentle caress, an exploration. *Oh, yes.* This is the kind of man who'll take his time. Desire unfurls deep within my belly. My fingers spear through the soft hair at the nape of his neck, keeping him close, nearly swooning with the delicious feeling of rough scruff and velvety lips.

He breaks the kiss, his thumb stroking over my lower lip. "I have to go to my friend's place now. Tonight?"

I nod and then grab his head, seeking more. He smiles against my lips, his strong arm binding around my waist, anchoring me against him. His kiss is hungry, demanding, promising more. My legs go weak, and I cling to his shoulders. I dimly hear the sound of bags dropping to the sidewalk.

He lifts his head, looking as dazed as I feel. "How about we meet at the bar of my hotel?"

I bite my lower lip, considering saying we could skip the drink and go to his room. Is that too forward? Lust is at an all-time high at the moment. I know what I want, and it's *not* a drink.

He steps back and hands me the gift bag with my giraffe. "No pressure." He rattles off the name of his hotel, not far from the convention center. "Let me give you my number too."

I smile, determined to keep this time with him as no-strings as possible. It's the only way no one gets hurt. "No need. I know the place."

He grabs his bag from the sidewalk and cocks his head. "If I don't see you again, I've enjoyed our time together very much."

I watch him walk away, a little surprised at his sweetness. Wait, he doesn't believe I'll meet him tonight. How could he not believe me after the most sensual kiss of my life?

"Me too!" I call after him. "I'll see you at eight o'clock at the hotel bar."

He turns around, smiling, sending a rush of adrenaline through me. "Okay, miss...I don't even know your last name."

"No last names. See you at eight."

"Make it seven."

My stomach flutters. "Seven it is."

"You keep looking at me like that, and I won't be able to stop kissing you, right here on this sidewalk."

I laugh. "Go. There's a baby out there who needs to be squeezed into that pouch you bought."

With one last smile, he puts a hand up in farewell and walks to his car, a red Ford Mustang. *Nice rental.*

I pull open the door to my car, get in, and just sit there for a moment, my mind spinning. I met a guy who makes my heart race and my insides turn upside down. That would make a good meet-cute in a romantic comedy. Too bad I don't write those. I never could believe in the happy ending.

Still...I smile widely, my stomach doing a flip as I think of Dominic. I can't wait for tonight.

2

Dominic

A beautiful woman cuddling a kitten is catnip for a veterinarian, but it was more than that. It was the way she looked at me, like she was wild for me, like I was someone important. It made me feel like a man instead of the divorced guy people feel sorry for when they hear how my ex-wife screwed me over. I haven't had a relationship in the three years since our divorce. I lost faith that a good woman existed, someone you could count on for the long haul.

The strange thing is, Eve seemed so familiar to me, something about her face. I'm not sure why. She's beautiful—tall with dirty-blonde hair cut at her jawline, sharp cheekbones, and lush lips. Maybe I've seen her in a modeling ad or on TV. Anything's possible in LA. All I know is I can't wait for tonight.

I just hope she shows up. She was careful to manage some distance, not even taking my number. Makes me wonder if she's coming off a bitter divorce too. My ex-wife, Lexi, left me for a wealthy investment banker, who happens to be her sister's ex-husband. It gets worse. The day she left, she informed me she was pregnant with *his* baby. I was in shock and didn't ask any questions, just said goodbye. My jaw clenches thinking about it. She blew up our marriage and her family. Her sister was furious, of course.

If tonight happens with Eve, it's just pure sexy fun, and maybe that's for the best. We both know the score, so no one will get hurt. I've got a lot going on in my life and very little free time with the veterinary practice I took over and the animal shelter I started next door to it.

I ring the doorbell at my friend's ranch-style house with a neat yard in a nice neighborhood of LA. The door swings open to Brian, a guy I met during my time in the Marines. He looks good, tanned and fit. His blond hair is still cut military short.

"Dr. Russo," he says in a mock formal voice.

"Yeah, yeah. Congrats, man." I hand him the gift bag of baby stuff. He takes it and gives me a one-armed bro hug.

"Good to see ya, Dom. The baby's taking a nap."

I step inside. His wife, Connie, greets me warmly, giving me a kiss on the cheek. She's a petite Mexican American woman with long dark brown hair and dark brown eyes. She met Brian when he started college in LA after his military service. "Thanks for coming all this way."

I lift a shoulder. "Wish I could make it out here more often. I was in town for a veterinary conference."

"Can you believe this guy?" Brian says, hitching a thumb at me. "Marines to veterinary school. Who would've thought?"

"And you went from the Marines to Hollywood," I say. "Who would've thunk it?"

He laughs. "I'm a camera operator, not a movie star. How's your knee? We'd better get you seated." He gestures toward a cushy-looking green sofa in the living room.

"My knee's fine." I was medically discharged from the Marines after I blew out my knee, or I should say shrapnel did. I can walk on it just fine, but I couldn't get back to fighting Marine form. "Wish I could've stayed in with you and the guys, but I'm happy being a vet."

"Twice a vet," Connie says with a laugh. "A vet who's a vet. Can I get you a drink?"

"I'll get it, babe," Brian says. "You need your rest." He turns to me, shaking his head. "Newborns keep you up round the clock. Water, beer, iced tea?"

"I'll take water, thanks." I follow him to the kitchen. "How's work?"

He pours me a glass of water. "Work's going well. There's a real sense of camaraderie on set. Not as tight as we were in the Marines, but still. I like that kind of environment. How's life treating you in New York? What was the name of that town you moved to? Sunnyville?"

"Summerdale," I say, taking the glass of water from him. He pours a second glass for Connie, and we return to the living room.

Brian sits in a leather recliner, so I sit on the sofa with his wife. He gestures toward me. "It sounds like you're doing great work with the shelter and the therapy dog program for vets."

I lift a palm. "I can't take all the credit. It's already an established program, Best Friends Care. I'm just running a chapter of it."

"Still."

A cry goes up from a back bedroom, and Connie leaps up, hurrying toward the baby.

"She's breastfeeding, so the moment Jaden cries, her milk lets down," Brian confides.

He always was one of the most down-to-earth guys I've ever met. He grew up on a dairy farm in Wisconsin. I'm from Michigan. I moved to New York for veterinary school; then I met my ex and stayed. There was a time when Lexi looked at me like I was her world. She showed her true colors after we were married. I tried to make it work out of loyalty. That sure backfired.

"You getting used to being a dad?" I ask.

That gets him talking for a long while on baby care from

swaddling to diaper changing. He sounds like an expert after only three weeks.

"That's great," I say when he winds down.

"Have you met anyone in New York?" he asks.

"Sure. Lots of people."

"You know what I mean. Post-Lexi action."

"I'm really busy with my practice and the animal shelter."

"Dom, you can't let her hold you back forever."

I shift in my seat. "I'm not."

"You haven't dated anyone significant since the divorce. What's it been?" He thinks for a moment. "Three years now. You're missing prime mating time. Get out there, man, before you lose your hair."

I self-consciously run a hand through my short thick hair. "I'm not losing my hair."

"You sure it's not thinning up there?"

"Stop," Connie says, coming back into the room with a tiny bundle in her arms. "Your hair is perfect, Dominic. Brian wishes he had your thick hair." She sits next to me on the sofa. The baby is swaddled in a striped blanket, wearing a cap with a pattern of playful puppies on it. Tufts of dark hair peek out of the cap. I'm surprised because I thought babies were born bald.

"Look at all that hair," I say.

She holds him against her chest and smiles down at him. "The babies in my family are always born with a head of hair."

"It sticks straight up," Brian says, gesturing over his head.

"Would you like to hold him?" Connie asks, smiling at me like it's a great honor.

I nod, holding my arms out. I've held newborn puppies and kittens before, but never a baby. I take him and settle him against my chest. A sense of wonder steals through me at this tiny human. The warm weight of his body, his tiny fingers curled into tiny fists, the little tufts of dark hair.

He lifts his head with effort, his brown eyes staring into mine. My heart shifts in that moment, opening in a way I haven't allowed in years. A sharp pang of raw longing hits, followed immediately by regret. It kills me that I missed out on this. It should've been me, Lexi, and our own baby. I can never get that back.

"He's amazing," I say hoarsely.

Eve

"Oh my God, Jenna, he's *amazing*!" I stare at my newborn nephew on my phone screen. Jenna just called as I arrived at the entrance to Dominic's hotel. I take a few steps away from the door and run a shaky hand through my hair, a lump of emotion caught in my throat. I had no idea I would take my nephew's arrival so personally. It's just that Jenna's kept me in the loop for her entire pregnancy. It almost felt like my pregnancy too, a vicarious excitement. "I'm an aunt!"

"And I'm a mommy!" She kisses his chubby cheek. Her husband, Eli, must be holding the phone to show them both off. Jenna looks good, her blond hair up in a ponytail, her skin glowing.

"Oh, I can't wait to meet him. My flight gets in late tomorrow night your time. I'll be at your place the next morning, or will you still be at the hospital?"

"What day is it today? I lost track of time when labor hit."

"Sunday."

"I'm hoping to check out by Tuesday morning at the latest. I always sleep better in my own bed. I'll let you know." She reaches out to take the phone and holds it up to the baby's hand. "Look at his tiny fingers."

I put a hand over my heart. Of course I know what babies look like, but this one is different. He's my nephew. His face comes back into view, and he yawns. Such a tiny little nose, and his lips are pursed like a rosebud. "Aww." My eyes well.

"I know," she says. "I can't believe we made him. Theodore Robinson, we made you."

Theodore yawns again.

"Are you going to call him Theodore or Teddy?"

"Theo," she says. "He's falling asleep. The nurse says I should sleep when he sleeps. Text me when you land tomorrow."

"I will. Love you guys!"

"Love you too."

Her husband, Eli, pops into the frame, a clean-cut, dark-haired cop with a heart of gold. Sometimes I wonder if Jenna got the last good one. "Safe travels, Eve."

"Thanks, see you soon." I disconnect, choked up, my eyes hot. I shake my head at myself. I'm not usually so emotional. I just have this intense longing to hold my vicarious baby. I never thought I'd get baby fever.

Deep breath. I can't show up for my fling all teary-eyed over a baby. A few more deep breaths later, I step into the lobby, heading for the hotel bar done in sleek metal with blue accents.

I do a quick scan of the bar, finding a few couples and a lot of empty chairs. It's Sunday night, so that's to be expected. I don't see Dominic. Was I stood up? Seriously, is it so hard for a man to show up when he says he will?

I take a slow scan of the entire lobby, and my stomach drops. He's not here. Well, this sucks. I was actually excited to see him again.

"Eve!"

I whirl, spotting Dominic striding toward me from the elevators. He moves with easy masculine grace, sure of himself. My pulse thrums through my veins.

He flashes a smile that lights up his face. "Had to take a shower after a baby mishap."

He reaches me, touches my arm lightly, and leans down to kiss my cheek. My breathing accelerates, my heart kicking harder.

"What happened?" I ask.

He places a hand on the small of my back, a warm imprint through the thin material of my red dress. "I went to visit my friend and his new baby. I was holding him. The baby, I mean." I laugh. "He spit up on me."

"Gross."

"Yeah, so I thought it best to shower and change. I'm used to a quick shower after dealing with animals all day."

We take a seat at the bar. The bartender, a young blond guy, comes over right away, setting coasters down in front of us. "What can I get you?"

"Sparkling water for me," I say.

"I'll have the same," Dominic says.

I give him a sideways glance as I arrange my dress over my knees. He's dressed nice in a light blue button-down shirt with the sleeves rolled up, revealing muscular forearms with a smattering of hair. He smells so good, clean and something distinctly him.

My phone chimes with a text. I smile widely at a photo of Theo that Eli just sent. My nephew's sporting a blue-striped cap, swaddled in a blue blanket. The text on the bottom of the picture has his name, length, and weight. Eli's obviously a proud dad. I show Dominic the picture.

He smiles. "Now there's a baby who'd love a stuffed giraffe. He can take it by the head and swing it around like a sword."

I laugh. "You got all that from his squishy-faced picture?"

"I have two younger brothers. Most anything can be used as a sword, but the long giraffe neck is ideal."

Our sparkling waters arrive with a wedge of lime. I squeeze my lime in before taking a sip. "You don't drink?"

"I figured since you weren't, I wouldn't either."

"Feel free to order whatever you like. I don't like my senses to be dulled before *you know*." Also, I prefer to remain stone-cold sober around men to avoid making poor decisions. I'll have an occasional drink with other women. Hard alcohol and any kind of drug stronger than Tylenol remain off-limits.

He gives me a slow sexy smile and inclines his head. "Fair enough. I'm not much of a drinker anyway. Just a beer once in a while."

Another for the plus column. After my history with men, including marrying my drug dealer, I now look for a man who makes healthy life choices. Though I already had a gut instinct that Dominic takes good care of himself. He's a virile, vibrant sort of man. Boy, he really brings out my alliterative flair.

Chill, he's your one-night guy, a way to test yourself. That's all. If the longing for a man goes away after we hook up, then I'll know that's all I needed. And there's nothing wrong with enjoying good sex once in a while.

I open my purse and pull some cash from my wallet. "Here you go, for the giraffe loan you gave me earlier. Did your friend's baby like the giraffe?"

He shakes his head. "No need to pay me back."

"Dominic, I insist." I lower my voice, leaning close. "No strings, no debts, no ties. I think we both know we're not going to see each other after tonight, right?" I hope that didn't sound too blunt. "You said you fly home tomorrow," I add. "I'm rooted here with my TV writer job. It's easier this way, so no one gets hurt."

The last thing I want is to play the *will he text me afterward* game. A clean break is best.

"Right, of course." He takes the money. "Hard to say if Jaden liked his giraffe. He didn't react much to it. He's only three weeks old."

"Give him a few more weeks. Or months. I don't know much about babies."

He pulls his phone out to show me a picture of him holding the baby, and my ovaries squeeze at the sweetness and all that dad potential. I swear I never considered dad potential in a guy before. I definitely have baby fever. Hopefully, hanging with my nephew will give me my fix because I have no idea if I'll ever get married again, let alone have kids. There's another close-up picture of the baby's face. His black hair sticks straight up.

"Look at all that hair!" I exclaim.

He smiles, looking at the picture. "I said the same thing.

Runs in the family, according to his mom. I had to get a picture."

"You look like a natural holding him. Are you experienced with babies?"

"No." He looks at the picture again, a wistful look coming over his face. "Different feeling than a puppy or kitten, that's for sure." He puts his phone away, takes a sip of sparkling water, and studies me for a long moment. "Are you famous? I'm not always up on celebrity stuff."

I laugh. "You don't have to use a line on me. I'm already in."

"No line, seriously. It's just that you look so familiar. This is LA. Actors and models as far as the eye can see."

A faint blush creeps up my cheeks at the compliment. "No, I'm not famous."

He leans close, smiling, his blue eyes sparkling with good humor. "Sure?"

I can't resist. I place my hand on his scruffy jaw, feeling the soft texture of whiskers over his square jaw. I lift my gaze to find a hunger in his eyes. My breath hitches.

I lean in and gently press my lips to his. A zing at contact has me pulling back to check in with him, a question lingering in the air between us. *Still fantastic chemistry. Can we go upstairs now?*

"Well," I say in a breathy voice.

His hand curls around the back of my neck, drawing me close for another kiss. His lips move expertly over mine, not too firm, just right. Time stops. There's nothing but the heat of the kiss, the dizzying sensation of falling into a pool of sensation. His tongue spears into my mouth, the kiss turning carnal. My stomach flutters, and an ache, lower still, makes me want to get closer, skin on skin.

He breaks the kiss, resting his forehead on mine. His breathing is as unsteady as mine.

"Should we go upstairs now?" I ask.

3

He stands, tosses the cash I gave him on the bar, which is a huge tip, and offers his hand. I take it and stand indecently close to him. Oh, yeah, he wants me as much as I want him. I can feel the proof.

"I don't usually do this so soon after meeting someone," he says.

"Me either," I lie, practically skipping to the elevator with him. This is going to be awesome. Once lust has taken over, my busy mind shuts down. Thank God, or I'd never enjoy myself.

He presses the button for the elevator, his gaze eating me up. "There's just something about you."

"It's chemistry. Random, rare, and really awesome." I'm getting alliterative again in my excitement.

"Chemistry," he echoes softly. "I guess."

We step into the elevator, and it's just us in here. As soon as he hits the button for his floor, I throw myself at him, wrapping my arms around his neck and kissing him eagerly. It's even better than before. This time his hands roam all over me, his mouth as eager as mine, seeking more. He turns and pins me against the wall, lifting my leg and pressing his hardness against me. A thrill of white-hot pleasure floods me. It's been too long.

He shifts, his mouth trailing along the column of my neck, his teeth scraping against me. I shiver, electric tingles racing through me. He caresses my breasts, grazing lightly across my nipples. I moan softly, aching to feel more of him. I stroke over his massive erection, and he jerks away.

"What's wrong?" I ask.

He holds up a finger. "I'm way too turned on. Plus, we're in an elevator."

I smile and kiss along his throat before gently biting the side of his neck.

He moans. "Eve, what you do to me. Hold that thought."

"For how long?"

"At least until I get you into bed." But his hand roams down my spine and then cups my ass, keeping me tight against him. "God, I want you."

I nip his bottom lip and kiss him again.

The elevator dings for his floor, and he grabs my hand. We race to his room, laughing. It's not often you find someone who really clicks with you. At least in the sexy way.

The moment we get into the room, we slam together again, mouths fused, hands stroking, squeezing, caressing. He backs me up toward the bed and lowers me under him. His hands are a marvel of dexterity, stripping me out of my dress, bra, and panties while kissing me feverishly.

I scoot back, naked on the bed. "Condoms are in my purse. I dropped it by the door."

"I've got some on the nightstand. I was really hoping you'd show up."

I glance over at the proof and turn back to him, running my tongue over my top lip. "Strip nice and slow."

One corner of his mouth lifts. He obliges, slowly unbuttoning his shirt to reveal a hard muscular chest with *ridges* along his abs and a V leading to the bulge of my future pleasure. So sexy.

"I like it." I twirl my finger in the air. "Let's see the back view."

He turns and looks at me over his shoulder. Oh yes, I'm

liking the broad shoulders and powerful-looking back. Work-outs? Lifting animals all day? Don't care how he got it, I want it.

He turns back to me, slowly unbuttoning his jeans and carefully easing them over his massive erection.

"Keep going," I say in a husky voice, spreading my legs wide to give him some enticement.

He quickly sheds the jeans and boxer briefs, then shoes and socks, his eyes glued to me. He joins me on the bed, covering me, fitting himself between my legs. *Yes!* I grab a condom from the nightstand and hand it to him.

Dominic has other ideas, though, leaving the condom on the mattress next to me in favor of focusing on me. He kisses all over my face, soft brushes that heat my skin, gentle bites along the column of my throat. I was right. This is a man who takes his time. If only I weren't so revved up already. I want with a shocking intensity.

He shifts, kissing his way down my body, inch by slow inch, eventually kissing and suckling one breast, then the other. Each insistent tug is a direct line of pleasure to my sex.

I lift my hips. "I'm ready."

"There's no rush."

I'd hoped he'd take his time, but now that we're in the moment, I've waited long enough. Our bodies were meant to join. I need it like my next breath.

"Please," I say. "I ache for you."

His fingers delve between my legs, and I gasp at the shock of pleasure. His mouth covers mine, swallowing my soft moans as his fingers work magic. I tense, nearly at my peak, when he suddenly stops.

"I was so close," I protest.

"Not yet," he says, and then lowers himself down my body, his eyes locked on mine.

My breathing is erratic, my stomach fluttering, heart thundering.

"Relax," he says in a husky voice. "This could take a while."

"I can't take much—" I gasp as he tastes me. He licks, kisses, nibbles. Everything feels so good, but it's not enough. My hips rock against him mindlessly. He slides a finger inside me and then another, filling the empty ache. My body clutches around the invasion. He strokes me on the inside as his tongue laps at me, pushing me on and on.

And then his fingers shift, hitting a spot on the inside that has me bucking wildly and crying out. He clamps a hand on my hip, holding me in place for the sweet torture. I pant, trembling on the sharp edge of release. My world goes dark, and then bursts of starlight appear as I shudder in release, the orgasm ripping through me. Wave after wave of pleasure washes over me as he gentles, staying with me until I go limp.

"Mmph," I say by way of *thank you*. Speech eludes me.

He climbs up my body, smiling down at me. "You okay?"

I grab his head and kiss him soundly. "Yes."

He rolls the condom on and eases inside me. My breath shudders out with the delicious feeling of being filled by his thick length. And then he starts to move, every stroke bringing more pleasure. He tips my hips up, going deeper, and we both gasp.

He lifts his head, gazing into my eyes with such tenderness I stop breathing. My lips part in shock as emotion clogs my throat. No man has ever looked at me like this before. It's like he reached inside and squeezed my heart.

No, no, no. He was supposed to be my sex test, not make me *feel* something. At least not something this powerful. I thought maybe after he left, I'd have that familiar longing for more. Not this. Not now with a man who's flying home tomorrow.

My breathing is shallow, but I can't seem to look away, caught under his spell.

He strokes my hair back from my face. "Eve, what you do to me."

I close my eyes, a defense against the unexpected intimacy. "More, faster, harder," I order.

He dips his head, biting gently along my neck, bringing

sharp rushes of sensation. And then he starts a slow roll, filling me to the hilt, each grind pressing exactly where I need him, each thrust hitting my G-spot, white-hot pleasure firing through me. Over and over and over. I surrender to the overwhelming sensations, riding higher and higher.

I keen, my head thrown back, as another release rockets through my body, only dimly aware of his low groan as he surrenders to his own pleasure.

We lie there panting for long moments. My limbs feel shaky, my body unused to the riot of sensations. He pulls out and lies next to me on his side, pulling me up against him. I'm too weak to protest cuddling, even though I know I should roll out of this bed, get my clothes on, and go home. I can't let myself get attached.

He kisses my hair. "Stay the night. I'm not done with you yet."

I press my lips together to keep from smiling. I'm ridiculously happy he wants me to spend the entire night. Is it all that emotion that sprang up from the way he looked at me that's making me nearly giddy? Maybe I'm just in a weird place with the arrival of my nephew and all the love I feel for him already.

He lifts my chin. "Okay?"

I force a straight face. "On one condition."

"Name it."

"You take me doggy style. A veterinarian would be good at that."

He rolls on top of me and tickles me. I giggle, squirming under him. No one ever tickles me.

He bites my earlobe and gives it a tug. His voice is husky by my ear. "What're you saying, I'm like an animal?"

I grin. "I hope so."

He kisses me, and I can feel his smile against my lips. One night. I'm going to make the most of it. Goodbye can wait a bit longer.

～

"Thank God you're here! I'm so overwhelmed!" Jenna hugs me like I'm her very last hope. I'm finally in Summerdale, New York, and sisters reunited is the best thing ever.

I drop my purse and the gift bag and throw my arms around her. Poor Jenna. Less than forty-eight hours of being a mom and she's already overwhelmed. This from a woman who runs a bakery, volunteers for many town committees and the local animal shelter, and is the best wife, caring friend, and sister in the world. Being a mom must be so hard.

Her two pit bull dogs, Lucy and Mocha, race around us, dropping their toys at our feet. Jenna kicks an orange fireman hose toy toward the dining room, and the dogs sprint after it.

She rocks me side to side as we hug. "I missed you! It's been too long."

"I missed you too!" I didn't realize how much I missed her until this moment, hugging in the foyer. My eyes sting, a happy lightness filling my body.

After my night with Dominic, I took a Monday afternoon flight and got in late last night. I didn't want to disturb Jenna at night with the baby, so I checked into a hotel and stopped by her place the next morning. With travel and the time difference, I'm already at less than a week with her—Tuesday to Sunday. Unfortunately, Monday afternoon was the earliest flight I could get after I found out she was in labor on Sunday. Damn this long distance.

Every reunion with my big sister feels like a huge deal because of all the years we missed out on from the split custody we went through and subsequent bad blood between our parents. Now it's like coming home to the happiest home I've ever known. We've made up for lost time over the last two years. I'm not especially close with my parents, and they weren't close with their parents either, on account of Mom dropping out of college her freshman year because she was pregnant with Jenna. It feels like a very tiny family of just me and Jenna. And now Theo and Eli too. Can't forget them.

She pulls back and wipes her eyes. I sniffle and wipe my eyes too.

"Why're you crying?" she asks with a watery laugh. "I'm the one overrun by hormones and lack of sleep."

"Because it's our sisters' reunion."

She hugs me again and kisses my hair. "I'm so glad you're in my life again."

We pull apart, both of us taking deep breaths in an attempt to calm down. Neither of us is normally super emotional. I'm reserved, and I'd best describe Jenna as snarky.

"Please don't mind my haggard appearance," she says, gesturing vaguely at herself. "I was up every two hours last night with Theo and haven't managed a shower yet. We only got home an hour ago. Two nights at the hospital was all I could take. The doctor gave us the all clear."

"You look beautiful," I say dutifully. She has bags under her eyes, and she's wearing a T-shirt and sweatpants, but otherwise looks like her usual self. We resemble each other with dirty blond hair, both of us tall and lean. She's got green eyes, which I always thought were so pretty.

She rolls her eyes. "Right." She walks over to the gray sectional sofa and gingerly sits down.

I wince in sympathy and sit next to her. I've heard childbirth can be rough on the undercarriage. "Is the baby sleeping? It's so quiet."

"Oh, no. He doesn't like sleeping. Eli took him on a walk. Theo's bundled in this little pouch sling that recreates the security of the womb."

That makes me think of Dominic, who bought a pouch for his friend's baby. I can't get him out of my head, constantly replaying our night together and before that too, the way we met, how sweet he was to pay for my giraffe toy, our first kiss on the sidewalk. My chest aches. Is it possible to miss someone you only knew for one day?

Reality check! You don't know how to get in touch, and he probably lives far from LA since he had to fly to get home.

Maybe this longing for more means I want more than good—hell, it was phenomenal—sex once in a while. I just need to gather the courage to put myself out there again. No rush. Next time I'll look for a guy like Dominic.

"Eve?"

I snap to attention. "Sorry, still a little jetlagged. I didn't think you'd be overwhelmed so soon. You're surrounded by family and friends." Eli has a large family in town, including an older sister, Sydney, who's Jenna's best friend.

She holds up a finger. "Eli's brothers don't know how to help with a baby. Sydney has her hands full with her eight-month-old, and she's pregnant *again*, battling terrible morning sickness. I'm not supposed to tell anyone. This was a surprise pregnancy."

"Wow. That's really close together."

She lifts one shoulder. "This is why I'm insisting on birth control if and when I ever manage to have sex again." She winces and shifts uncomfortably.

"Was the birth difficult for you?"

"It wasn't easy, I'll tell you that. Even knowing what to expect from our birthing class." She scrunches her face. "There was tearing, and I needed stitches."

Bile rises in my throat. I cross my legs in sympathy.

She nods. "The things you never wanted to know, or experience for that matter."

"What can I get you? You know I know nothing about babies. I'm here to take care of you."

"You think *I* know? I needed a lactation specialist at the hospital to show me how to nurse him. Basic feeding, and I had no clue."

I give her arm a squeeze. "In the old days, there was probably always a more experienced woman to help new moms, don't you think?"

She throws her hands up. "He cries, and I don't know what he wants. I'm guessing he wants to be fed or changed. Eli says sometimes Theo just wants to chill, but needs help getting there." Eli's the chief of police in town and a good guy. We were in the same grade in school. I lived in

Summerdale before the divorce, and a lot of people I grew up with moved back.

"Speaking of chilling." I grab my purse and gift bag from where I dropped them in the foyer and join her again. "For Theo." I hand her the gift bag, though it's obvious what it is because the giraffe head sticks out.

She smiles, her eyes watering. "Aww, cute."

I dig through my purse for the last-minute airport gift I got her. "And some chocolate for you." It's a slim box with a variety of chocolate candies.

She sets the giraffe on the sofa next to her and opens up the candy box, offering it to me.

"No, thanks. It's all for you."

"You're the best." She puts an entire chocolate truffle in her mouth and chews, looking blissful. At least I gave her a little bit of joy in this overwhelming time.

Lucy, a light brown pit bull mix, cruises the sofa, eyeing the giraffe.

"Lucy, no," Jenna commands. "Go get your ball."

Lucy runs off to a box of toys. Mocha beats her to it, grabbing a tennis ball and trotting over, dropping it at Jenna's feet. Jenna slouches deeper into the sofa, the box of chocolates resting on her belly. I toss the ball for Mocha, and both dogs take off after it.

"I didn't know what to get for a baby present," I say. "It seemed like a giraffe could be for a boy or girl."

"Sure. Anyway, I don't believe in toys that are just for a boy or a girl. I'm going to give Theo a doll to play with along with a truck." She pops another candy in her mouth and closes the candy box. "Can I get you anything?"

"How about I get you something? Or you could go lie down if you'd like."

"I'm supposed to drink extra water, thanks." She stretches out on the sofa, propping a pillow behind her.

I go to the kitchen, which has a sink full of dirty dishes and assorted baby gear scattered on the counter—bottles and caps, a sterilizer, a breast pump, pacifiers still in their packages, and a pile of soft-looking white cloths. Burp rags? Cloth diapers? No idea. I find a couple of glasses and get us both water.

I return to the living room, and she sits up. "Thank you." She drinks her water right away.

I take a seat on the chaise lounge end of the sectional sofa to give her room to stretch out if she wants. "I'm all yours until Sunday afternoon. I have to go back to work Monday morning."

She frowns. "I wish you could stay longer."

"Me too. I was lucky to get time off, though. We're only halfway through the season, so I'm needed. With the travel time and time difference, this was the best I could do."

"If only we lived closer to each other."

"You're welcome to join me in sunny California."

"I've got the bakery. Eli's chief of police, and his entire family is here."

We've had this conversation before. Now that we reconnected, it's tough to be so far away from each other. When you write for TV, LA's the place to be. It's a collaborative process in the writers' room.

I sigh. "I know, we're both tied to where we're at. So what kind of help are you getting with the baby?"

"Eli's entire family stopped by yesterday to check out Theo. Then Audrey organized a food chain to bring us dinner every night for the next week." Audrey is one of her best friends. Jenna was lucky enough to grow up with three girls who were like sisters to her. I had one best friend who stabbed me in the back in high school, devastating me. I couldn't wait to leave for college in California. Not that I'm bitter. It all worked out.

Jenna continues, "I'm afraid after the first week of help, I'll be on my own. You're leaving, Eli has to go back to work, and the food chain ends."

"I'll make sure you have some meals packed in your freezer. Will Mom be stopping by to help?"

Jenna scowls. "I don't want her help."

I've forgiven our parents for the trauma of their two-year-long divorce and splitting of our family. *Thank you, therapy.* Jenna's still working on it. She's pissed that our parents are living together again, proclaiming themselves to be in love. They even planned a wedding, but Mom chickened out at the last minute, leaving Dad at the altar. Insert eye roll here. Still, they stayed together. I'm of the opinion that they're adults and can do what they want. It doesn't affect me anymore.

"You told them about Theo, right?" I ask.

"Yeah, they'll be here on Saturday to visit. I'm so glad you'll be here as a buffer."

"I have a feeling Theo will be the bigger buffer. They'll be so enthralled with their first grandchild, it'll be a completely drama-free visit."

The front door opens, and Eli steps in, wearing Theo in a blue pouch sling on his chest. I can't even see the baby, only his outline.

"Hey, Eve!" Eli says cheerfully, walking over to me. He's uber fit and clean-shaven with short brown hair and warm hazel eyes.

I pop up from my chair. "Hey, new dad! Is the baby sleeping?"

"Yeah." He pulls back the fabric of the sling to show Theo curled up in there, his tiny fist next to his chubby cheek. I suck in air. He probably slept just like this in the womb.

I touch his tiny hand and whisper, "He's even more beautiful in person."

"Thanks," Eli says. "They told us at the hospital not to worry about lowering our voices. Babies get used to the sounds of the house."

I marvel at my nephew looking so angelic. "Hi, Theo, it's your aunt Eve. I'm so glad you're here."

Eli turns to Jenna. "How're you doing?"

"Tired, sore, overwhelmed."

"Sounds like me, minus the soreness. You want that donut cushion?"

She waves that away. "No. I'm just going to lie down here while Eve entertains me with stories of Hollywood."

Eli turns to me. "Jenna told me you're at a hotel. We have a guest room set up for you upstairs. Why don't you move your stuff over here?"

"You have to," Jenna says, sounding more like herself. "You always did before."

"I know, but I didn't want you worrying about a guest when you're taking care of a newborn."

"You're not a guest, you're family," Eli says.

"Exactly," Jenna says.

My eyes get hot. It's just so nice to feel like I'm part of the family. "Okay, I have to get back to the hotel by eleven to check out, and then I'll bring my stuff back here."

Jenna smiles, satisfied, and reclines on the sofa again. Eli tucks a pillow under her knees and then drops a kiss on her forehead. She kisses him on the lips and peeks into the sling to admire Theo, reaching in to touch him, and then lies back, looking satisfied.

"I'm going to put him in his crib," Eli says, heading upstairs.

I stretch out on the chaise lounge end of the sofa, and Jenna stretches out, poking my hip with her toes. "Did I mention I'm glad you're here?"

I laugh. "Yes. Me too."

A few moments later, we hear Eli's deep voice through a baby monitor on the coffee table. "You're the best baby in the world, did you know that? Yes, you are."

"God, I love him even more now," Jenna says, wiping tears from her eyes. "Eli is an amazing dad."

My own eyes well. Seeing Jenna with her husband and new son makes the whole family thing much more appealing. "You're so lucky."

"I know it. One day you'll meet a great guy too." She pauses. "Did you turn your profile back on for that dating app? I know you've been busy, but there's more to life than work. I want you to have love in your life too."

I shake my head. "But—"

"If you take a chance and open your heart, you might be surprised at how good things turn out. Don't let Mom and Dad's example hold you back. They're nuts."

I smile. "Actually, I did meet someone at the baby store of all places, but it wasn't meant to be. He was just in town for a conference."

"Where does he live? Maybe it's not that far, and you could visit each other."

I lift one shoulder up and down. "He had to take a flight home, so I imagine it wasn't close. Anyway, we both decided up front it was just one night of fun. No ties, no strings, so there's no messy expectations, and no one gets hurt."

I look away, feeling far from casual despite my words. Thoughts of Dominic tumble through my mind.

Sparkling sky-blue eyes.

His deep sexy voice. *Relax. This could take a while.*

The unexpected tenderness in his eyes when we were as close as two people could be.

I take a sip of water, swallowing over the lump in my throat. I'm not sure I'll ever meet a guy like Dominic again.

"Well, at least you had fun." She pauses. "How much fun?"

Jenna and I don't hold back on the details. Between us, it's a safe space for sharing *everything*.

I smile dreamily. "It was awesome. He knew what he was doing, and he took his time."

She sighs. "Don't you love when that happens? It's so rare."

"I know!"

She gives me a concerned-big-sister look—brows scrunched together, lips pursed. "And you're really okay with not having that again? Chemistry can be a great start. That's what Eli and I had at the beginning."

"This is completely different from you and Eli." Eli's a guy you can count on, a man who says what he means and shows up for you. It's what I secretly want for myself, though I have serious doubts about finding such a rare specimen. I don't believe in a happy ending where men are concerned. I've been burned too many times.

At her expectant look, I continue, "This guy wasn't looking for anything serious. Besides, I love the single life." I force enthusiasm into my voice, trying to convince her as well as myself. The truth is, I'm not ready for the relationship roller coaster. *Strap in as your stomach drops and your life careens out of control!*

Jenna keeps pushing. "I know, but—"

I cut her off. "Everything is exactly how I want it—great apartment, great job, friends, and the occasional fun night with a guy. I've got it all, Jenna. The twenty-nine-year-old bachelorette dream."

"What happens when you turn thirty?"

"I'm staying twenty-nine."

"Good call." She nudges me with her toe again. "Exactly how good was he?"

"Four orgasms in a night."

Her eyes half close, and she covers a yawn. "That is a beautiful thing."

"Right? Oh, I've got to tell you the latest with Ray." That's one of my co-writers. "He just got an iguana he's obsessed with." I go on telling her stories of the writers' room and the eccentricities of some of my coworkers. Within minutes, she falls asleep just like I thought she would.

I take a white fleece blanket from the top of the sofa and cover her with it. Even though I'm the younger sister, I feel protective of her. The sisterhood bond can't be broken. Not by years of estrangement, not by selfish parents, not by three thousand miles between us. My eyes sting as I take one last look at her before heading to the kitchen to wash dishes.

It's always hard to leave her after a visit. I imagine it'll be doubly hard to leave my nephew too. But that's reality.

I wish I could magically shrink the country so the East and West Coasts were commuting distance apart or invent teleportation or relocate Hollywood. *Imagination one, real life zero.*

4

I really thought I had zero maternal instinct, but within three days I'm so bonded with this baby I feel like a second mom to him. I'm starting to see how much I'd really like a child of my own. It's overwhelming to care for a helpless little human, like Jenna said, but it's also all kinds of wonderful. I never thought I could love a baby the way I love Theo.

Jenna says since we're sisters, we must have a similar scent that Theo recognizes. I don't know if that's true, but this sweet bundle of joy responds to me. He gazes into my eyes like an old soul. He calms when I hold him, and once he even tried to nurse on me. Ha. Sorry, buddy, no milk there.

A vision of Dominic holding his friend's baby comes to mind. He looked so natural and full of dad potential. I kinda wish I had a copy of that picture. Silly, I know, to include him in a fantasy future—a nice guy like that holding our baby. Reality is, I have no way of contacting him, he probably lives far away, and I still have a wall of fear separating me from a relationship. Nothing wrong with a fantasy though, right? It's safe and pleasant.

So far Theo only stares at the giraffe I bought him, but he doesn't reach for it. He much prefers to grab my hair whenever it swings with my movements. Boy, does he have a tight grip. It's tough to extricate my hair from his fist without losing some.

"It's going to be so hard to leave him," I tell Jenna on Friday morning. We're in the baby's room, and she's dressing him in a fresh blanket sleeper. This one is yellow with a pattern of monkeys in palm trees. Theo's legs and arms flail as she tries to get them into the sleeves and leg holes. I hold the fabric in place while she wrestles with him.

She glances at me. "Well, I'm not going to tell you to quit your job and stay here with me, but it would be nice."

"It's not always easy to get a good gig. The show's going strong. Everyone says it's going to get picked up for another season."

"Sure, sure, but does your boss know your sister had a baby?"

I grin. "How do you think I got a week off?"

She deftly does the snaps on Theo's sleeper. Less than a week and she's a pro at the tiny fasteners. "I have a favor to ask."

"Anything. I'm here for you."

"Thank you," she says in a choked voice. She scoops up Theo and cuddles him against her chest. When she turns to me, a tear leaks out of her eye. I wipe it away for her. "I so appreciate you taking time out of your busy schedule, flying across the country, putting up with interrupted sleep, taking care of me, Theo, cleaning up, just everything." More tears stream down her cheeks.

"Wow." I grab a tissue and gently dab the tears from her cheeks. "How long do these hormones last?"

She sniffles. "I have no idea. You know I'm not usually like this. I love you." She kisses Theo's cheek. "And you too, Theo."

"I love you too. And you, little baby." I stroke his soft cheek. "What's the favor? You want me to do the laundry and fold all these tiny baby things?"

"That would be awesome, but I was going to ask if you could help out with the fundraiser for the animal shelter tonight, and also tomorrow they'll need help at the tent with pets in need of adoption at the Fall Harvest Festival. I always pitch in for both." She bounces Theo a little as he starts to get fussy. "I had such a great experience when I adopted Mocha from Dr. Russo, and you know he's the best dog in the world."

"Everyone knows that. Of course I'll help."

"Great! Audrey will be there too. I'll text her and let her know to expect you."

She hands me Theo and pulls her phone from her back pocket. I relax instantly as his weight melts against me. I breathe in delicious new-baby smell and walk with him over to the window, singing to him about flying in an airplane to visit. Maybe one day he'll visit me too.

Audrey meets me in the parking lot of The Horseman Inn at seven that night. She's a sweet woman, a petite brunette with long straight hair, who runs the library. I've met her several times since she and Jenna are close.

"Hey, Audrey," I call.

She plants her hands on her hips. "So *you're* the one hogging all the baby time."

I cross to her and give her a hug. "You're welcome to visit Theo any time."

"I didn't want to interrupt sister bonding time. I know you've only got a week together. I'll be by to help after you go back to LA."

"So how've you been? The library keeping you busy?"

"That, and I wrote a book." She smiles shyly. "I don't usually tell people, but you're a writer, so I thought I'd share."

Jenna had already told me. She keeps me filled in on all the latest in Summerdale, but I keep that to myself. "Congratulations! You know, a lot of people say they want to write a book, but so few do. That's a big deal."

She blushes and pushes her hair behind her ears. "Thanks. It was…an experience. Kind of a roller coaster of being in love with it and pulling my hair out."

Just like a relationship. Writing is like that too, but at least I can control my scripts.

"Sounds about right. Now I can let you in on the secret writer hand signal." I pretend to type rapidly in the air and then lift my palms for a double high five.

She laughs and copies my typing gesture before slapping me five. "I'm in the club!"

"Are you sending it out to literary agents, or are you going to self-publish?"

She heads for the front door. "It's not ready for anyone to read. I need to give it a final polish."

"I'd be happy to read it when you're ready. What's it about?"

She holds the door open for me. "A military family saga. I wouldn't want to bother you with it. I know you're busy with the baby and your own writing."

"I could squeeze it in."

"Maybe. If I think it's ready, I'll keep you in mind."

We pass by the host desk, and Audrey explains why we're here. I glance over to the front dining room, where a bearded man carries a long table into the room. Another guy carries the other end of the table, his back to us. There's something familiar about his thick dark hair. The bearded guy too. Probably guys I knew when I was very young from town, who look different all grown up. A brunette woman with large glasses stands next to a pile of gift baskets wrapped in colorful cellophane with bows. She doesn't look familiar.

Audrey gestures to the busy back dining room, where one of the guys moving the table went to talk to someone. "Dr. Russo is our beloved veterinarian, and he runs this awesome animal shelter behind his office. They have a chapter of Best Friends Care too. That's the organization that trains shelter dogs to be therapy dogs for veterans with PTSD and other disabilities. Anyway, I've been volunteering more there since

I've gotten to know him better. He's helping with my cat Cinder's intestinal issues."

"That's good that Cinder's getting the care she needs." It's Friday night, and the back dining room is packed. It sounds like the bar is hopping too. The silent auction is supposed to happen in an hour, along with a trivia game with prizes, so the more people, the better. Jenna filled me in on the details earlier.

The bearded guy steps in front of me. "Hey, Aud. Evie, good to see you. It's been a long time." Evie is my childhood nickname, so he must be someone I knew as a kid.

I tilt my head, studying him. I can't place him. "It's Eve now."

Audrey pipes up, "That's Levi Appleton, our mayor."

My lips part in surprise. "I didn't recognize you with the beard. And mayor too."

"No one else wanted the job," Levi says with a smile.

The brunette woman with glasses joins us. "He's a great mayor, and he's venturing into filmmaking too."

"This is my girlfriend, Galena," Levi says.

"Hi, Galena," I say warmly before turning to Levi. "Interesting to hear you're getting into filmmaking. I write for a TV show. I got a week off to help Jenna with her baby."

"Audrey here's a writer too," Levi says.

I glance at Audrey, who looks uncomfortable. For someone who says she doesn't usually share about her book, it seems like the word is out. I bet not much stays private in a small town like Summerdale. "She told me about that."

The guy who looked vaguely familiar from behind heads toward us. I suck in air. My heart thunders in my ears. I know that face, that body, the easy confident stride. *Dominic.*

One-night-stand Dominic.

He lives here.

Ahhh!!!

Do I pretend I don't know him?

What do I do?

I blink a few times. My eyes are the only part of me functioning at the moment as they stare at him in lusty horror. The man I had the hottest sex of my life with is *here* in the dinky town of Summerdale, New York. What are the chances? Seriously!

He was supposed to stay a fantasy in my imagination!

My heart thunders, threatening to burst out of my chest. I never thought I'd see him again. *What do I do? What do I say?*

Dominic joins us. "More volunteers, I hope?" He stares at me, his eyes widening in sudden recognition.

Audrey gestures toward him. "Eve, meet Summerdale's most eligible bachelor."

My brows shoot up. *Most eligible bachelor? Are all the women in town after him?* "Hi."

"Hi." His voice sounds hoarse.

The pieces rapidly click in place in my mind. I'm here to help with a fundraiser for an animal shelter in town run by a veterinarian, whom Jenna works with frequently. Jenna's veterinarian is *my* veterinarian. Should I pretend we're meeting for the first time? The last thing I want is for him to think I followed him here in a weird stalker situation.

"What do you mean most eligible bachelor?" Galena asks Audrey. "I thought you were seeing each other."

Audrey's cheeks turn bright pink. I look away. *Awkward.* He's Audrey's boyfriend or ex-boyfriend.

Dominic glances at me before turning back to Galena. "Where did you hear that?"

Audrey answers for her. "Town gossip. Always someone pairing up someone. Ha-ha."

"Audrey and I are friends," Dominic says, looking right at me.

"Exactly," Audrey says with a nod.

Don't worry about me! Not my business what you do with women in your hometown, or anywhere, really. Can I go now? Oh, wait. I haven't done any work yet.

"But Levi said..." Galena trails off and turns to Levi, a question in her eyes.

Don't need to know; don't want to know.

I blow out a breath, looking around the room in a valiant effort not to stare at Dominic. "Right. Okay. I'm here in Jenna's place, so put me to work."

Dominic gestures for us to follow him toward a large box of decorations and signs.

Audrey tells me she'll set up the baskets on the table, so I look into the box and pull a few rolls of streamers out. I can feel Dominic's eyes on me. The hair on the back of my neck rises. I remember every minute from the moment we met until the moment we said goodbye. It's been playing like a movie in my head.

I grab some tape and get to work with shaking hands. I'm freaking out. I can admit it.

A few minutes later, I hear Dominic tell Levi and Galena they're off duty. Oh, great. Now it's just me, Audrey, and the sexiest man I've ever met. No repeat performance here. Don't even consider it, I tell my lustier parts. That way lies madness. I give myself a stern lecture: *He's from here, you're from LA, and you're not ready for whatever this is.*

You're leaving on Sunday!

I turn and wave bye to Levi and Galena. My gaze collides with Dominic's, his blue eyes smoldering into mine like he remembers every moment of that night too. I tear my gaze away. Act casual. It was only one night. We both agreed. Don't make things more complicated. I'm leaving on Sunday I nearly blurt out loud. Like anyone asked.

A warm hand touches my arm, and I instantly know it's him. I close my eyes, fighting the urge to melt against him. He speaks in a husky whisper near my ear. "What're you doing here?"

"I'm not stalking you," I say defensively. "It was one night just like we agreed."

Audrey gasps and shoots us a curious look.

∾

Dominic

All of my senses are on high alert. I can't believe she's here. Eve in Summerdale. She brushes her blond hair back from her face and looks away. When I finally said goodbye to her the morning after the best sex of my life, I told her I wanted to keep in touch. She kissed me and told me it was better to go out on a high note.

This whole week I kept replaying that night, wishing I had a way to get in touch with her again, and now she's *here*. It's a second chance for us.

"I never thought you were stalking me," I say. "I was just surprised to see you."

She worries her full lower lip. "My sister lives in town. Jenna Robinson. She's the one who just had the baby."

"Theo."

Her eyes go soft. "You remember."

"I remember everything about that night." My voice sounds husky.

She tucks her hands behind her. "Let's not go there."

Her sharp angular cheekbones and jaw, the color of her hair—it's just like Jenna. "I can't believe I didn't see it before, the resemblance to your sister. Your eyes are a different color than hers, but everything else is so similar. When we met, you looked vaguely familiar, and I thought it was because you were a model or actor, but it was because of Jenna."

She slowly shakes her head. "I told you I wasn't famous."

I pull my phone from my pocket. "Now that you're here, let me get your number."

She holds up a palm. "I don't think that's a good idea."

I step closer. "Eve, I haven't been able to get you out of my head."

"I'm leaving on Sunday. Let's not make this more difficult than it needs to be."

I press my lips together to keep from propositioning her. But what could it hurt to have one more night together? Or maybe see each other more regularly. Though long distance across the country would be tough. Maybe she's right.

She points toward the box of decorations. "I'll finish up

the decorations. Do you need help with the silent auction too? Cleanup? Or maybe help with the trivia game? Anything Jenna would do, I'm happy to do."

"Audrey's helping with the silent auction. I'm doing prizes. Wyatt, our sometimes bartender, is running the trivia game, so you could stick around for cleanup, or I could just do it myself."

She smiles tightly. "I'll stick around. And I'll jump in wherever I'm needed for the rest of the night. I'll be at the festival tomorrow helping with the animal adoption tent too. Jenna told me there's a raffle with gift certificates to her bakery to benefit the animal shelter."

"So I'll see you tomorrow too."

She wags her finger at me. "In a strictly professional capacity."

I smile. "I know your last name now. Eve Larsen. I knew Jenna before she married Eli."

"And you must be her beloved veterinarian Dr. Russo."

I bow. "At your service. Did Jenna say I was beloved?"

"Audrey said it. She's quite a fan of yours. Have you two ever…" She gestures vaguely. Audrey shifts to the other side of the room.

"No. I'm not sure why people thought we were together. We had drinks one night, but that's all."

"Small-town grapevine."

I rub my jaw. "That's what's odd. We met in Clover Park at the Happy Endings bar because she said she wanted a change of scenery. How did they hear about it here?"

She glances at Audrey. "Maybe she shared with her friends because she hoped it would be something more. She's sweet and still single."

I search her expression. *Does she remember that night in vivid detail the way I do?* "I'm not interested in sweet." *I want someone who excites me. I want you.*

"Too bad. You're missing out." And with that, she goes back to putting up decorations across the room.

I watch her for a few minutes before marching over to her. "Did that night mean nothing to you?"

She glances around and whispers, "Not here."

"Then where?"

She gestures for me to follow her, and walks out the front door. I follow her to a corner of the parking lot with a street-light overhead.

"We agreed it was one night, no strings," she says through her teeth.

"That was before. This is now."

"I'm here for less than forty-eight hours. Maybe you're lonely, I get it—"

"I'm not lonely. I'm the town's most eligible bachelor."

She rolls her eyes.

I lower my voice. "And I know how to pleasure you."

She jolts, but recovers quickly, parking a hand on her hip. "So you want a second night? Is that what you're after? Because I'm not here for booty calls. I'm here to help Jenna with the baby."

"The baby sleeps sometimes, right?"

She steps close, her eyes meeting mine. "Let me be clear. I'm not interested in another hookup that leads nowhere."

"Me either." My gut tightens, my pulse accelerating at having her so near.

It's not just lust, though the lust is powerful. She's the first woman to make me feel anything in a long time.

God, the way she looks at me.

She lifts a hand like she's going to touch my jaw, and then drops it. "Good. Glad we're on the same page. My next thing will be a real relationship. Not long distance, not a fantasy, well, maybe a fantasy until I'm ready. I'm not ready yet, and there's no rush." She nods once.

I stare at her, confused. "What do you think I'm asking for, a commitment?"

"No!" She throws her hands up. "I don't know. I just don't think you and I have a future, so..." Her gaze drops to my mouth, and her breath hitches. "I should go."

But she doesn't move away.

My heart thumps harder, every nerve ending at attention. "Fine. Don't give me your number. Don't spend another minute more with me than you have to."

"I wish I could forget you." Then she grabs my head and kisses me roughly. Raw lust surges through me. I wrap an arm around her waist, pulling her flush against me as I return the kiss with all the pent-up desire I've felt since the moment I left her in that hotel room. The kiss goes on and on, a fire reignited between us.

She breaks the kiss suddenly, her fingertips resting against her lips, her eyes soft. For a moment, she looks almost vulnerable. "I'm sorry." She hurries toward the restaurant.

I blow out a breath, tip my head back, and stare at the stars. I don't know what my goal is here. All I know is that I can't just forget what happened between us then or now.

I head back toward the restaurant, open the door, and collide with Eve on her way out.

"Sorry!" she exclaims and steps back. Her eyes meet mine. "Forget any of this ever happened, okay?"

She slips by me and heads toward her car.

"What if I don't want to forget?" I yell after her.

She gets in her car and peels out of the lot.

I stand there in a daze for a moment. She's not wrong. There's no future with us living on opposite coasts. Does that make her more appealing in some twisted way? No risk of permanent damage knowing there's a natural end.

I run a hand through my hair. What am I doing? I can't seem to think straight when it comes to Eve. All I know is for the first time since the divorce, I desperately want more.

Desperation is not good. No woman will ever have that power over me. My life is just fine. Great, even.

Dammit. I still don't have her number.

5

Eve

I sit in my car in Jenna's driveway, taking a few calming breaths while I try to reconcile my actions with my words. I pushed him away in every way I could, and then what did I do? Kiss him! That was all my doing. It was just that up close I remembered how electric it was between us, how tender he could be, the way he seemed to know how to amp things up at just the right time for an explosive orgasm.

I rest my forehead on the steering wheel. That's the problem here. A four-orgasm-night problem. If the sex hadn't been so mind-blowing, I wouldn't be tempted.

I sit up straight and push my hair out of my eyes. Except it's not just the sensual memories. He's smart, gorgeous, and tender. My sister and Audrey think he's awesome. There's no denying he's doing great work. Jenna told me how involved Dominic is in selecting therapy dogs to go to veterans. All signs point to a winner, a hero in every sense of the word.

But what am I supposed to do? Let myself get involved only to say goodbye after two days? I'll see him tomorrow at the Fall Harvest Festival, and I leave the next day. Bad enough my heart will be breaking to leave Theo and Jenna. Do I really need to add Dominic to the mix?

No, I do not. This whole thing was just a bizarre coincidence. I have a life back in LA. He's rooted here. End of story.

I pull my phone from my purse and text Audrey a teensy lie about Jenna needing me. She answers back with a cheery, *No problem! Dominic and I have it covered. I know the baby needs you more than we do.*

I let out a breath. Guess I should go inside and actually make good on my reason for leaving. I'll tell Jenna they didn't need me until tomorrow. I'm sure she'll be happy for the baby help.

My phone vibrates with a text. Oh shit. It's from my boss, Matt.

Writers' strike is official as of Monday morning. Looks like we all get more time off. Check your email for the details.

I slap a hand over my mouth. There'd been talk about a possible strike next summer before the new season's work began. This will bring everything to a screeching halt mid-season.

I click over to my email to read about the failed negotiations for the new contracts with the TV and film producers association. It's for percentage raises for the usual stuff, but also new forms of digital content. I press a hand to my head. The writers' union is counting on the unexpected mid-season strike to give them more leverage. The last time they went on strike—before I was in the industry—it lasted three months. That's a long time to go without a paycheck.

My thoughts bounce all over the place. How will I make rent? Most of my savings went toward making a film during my time off based on my original screenplay. Unfortunately, it didn't win any major film festivals, so it didn't get distribution. It was a story about sisters reunited loosely based on my life. Jenna loved it.

Do I get unemployment? A quick Google search nixes the unemployment benefits. Not for union strikers in California.

I read through the email from my boss. There's a possibility of a loan through my union if I'm in danger of losing housing or other catastrophic circumstances. Okay, there's a bit of a cushion *if* I get approved. My stomach rolls. I'm not liking the uncertainty of everything I thought was set in stone in my life.

Jenna appears in the driveway, waving to me through the car window.

I get out of the car, still dazed. "Hi."

"Are you okay? I heard you pull up, but you stayed in your car for so long I got worried. Are you not feeling well?"

"No, I'm fine. I, uh, helped decorate for the fundraiser, but they had enough people, so I came back here to help you out more."

She gives me a concerned look. "You look like you've had bad news. Come inside. I'll get you some tea."

"Is Theo sleeping?"

"Eli's pacing with him, attempting to get him to sleep. If it doesn't work, he's going to take him for a car ride. We're learning that reliably gets him to sleep. The problem is transferring him from the car to the crib without waking him up."

I follow her inside. "Hey, Eli."

Theo lets out a howl.

"Hey, Eve." Eli pats Theo's back. "It's okay, buddy. You're just overtired. Let's go for a drive."

"Check his diaper first," Jenna says.

Eli holds him up and sniffs him. "Good call. Changing time." He takes him upstairs.

Jenna goes to the kitchen, fills the teakettle, and sets it to boil. We both like chamomile tea for its calming effect.

I take a seat at the kitchen table. She joins me in the adjacent seat with a couple of napkins and a plate of chocolate-chip cookies that smell heavenly. She pushes the cookies toward me.

"Were you baking?" I ask.

"Yeah, it relaxes me. I'm used to baking for hours every day. My assistant is doing a great job in my absence at the bakery, but I miss it."

I pick up a cookie. It's still warm! I take a bite of soft

cookie with melting chocolate chips, closing my eyes in a moment of cookie ecstasy.

She laughs and takes a bite of her cookie. "My favorite comfort food."

"I could eat this whole plate of cookies. They're so good. No wonder you opened your own bakery. I still haven't tried everything there."

"There's a lot to try, and I change it seasonally. Now that it's fall, I'm going for pumpkin, cinnamon, and apple flavors. Winter goes heavy on the chocolate, peppermint, and gingerbread. Spring is lighter stuff with vanilla and fruit, and of course summer is my famous ice-cream-cake sandwiches. You've only been here for summer."

"Are the fudge brownies seasonal too?"

"I always have those. So-o-o, now that you've had a chance for the chocolate and sugar to do their happy-making thing, what's bothering you?"

I set my cookie down. "The writers' union went on strike as of Monday morning, so I'm officially out of work until a new contract is agreed upon with the TV and film producers association."

"You can stay longer!" she exclaims.

My lips part. I hadn't thought that far ahead. "I guess that's true."

She reaches for me with both hands, and I meet her halfway for a double-hand squeeze. "This is so exciting! I was just telling Eli how sad I was that you were leaving on Sunday. You just got here on Tuesday. It wasn't even a full week. And now you can stay...how long are writers' strikes?"

"I don't know. The last one was three months."

"You could be here for Theo's first Thanksgiving and his first Christmas too!"

"That would be cool," I say absently, my mind flashing to Dominic. He said he couldn't get me out of his head. If I stick around Summerdale, how can I resist him? Unlike LA, Summerdale is small enough that I could run into him multiple times.

Do I need to resist him? Could I let my fantasy relationship with a great guy like Dominic turn into something real?

But then I'd ultimately have to go back to my life in LA.

A natural end to a relationship makes it less scary in some ways, but it would lead to heartbreak. I don't want the anguish and tortured longing. I want what Jenna and Eli have —true love, no torture involved. Though it wasn't always smooth sailing for them, now it is. I'd like to jump to that part.

Am I actually starting to believe in a happy ending with a guy? My gut clenches at the thought. Not ready yet, but I'm starting to *want* to believe in a happy ending of my own. It's just not going to happen with Dominic because of these particular circumstances. Still, it's progress that I'm even considering it for my future. It's okay not to be ready, I reassure myself.

"I'm sorry," Jenna says. "Here I was all excited for what this could mean for me. You must be worried about being out of work."

"I am." And worried about resisting a ridiculously sexy veterinarian.

Clearly, that's the only safe route. It was the Jenna connection that brought us together, shopping for a baby at the same time, and now it's the Jenna connection keeping us in the same town. I'm not going to abandon Jenna just to avoid Dominic.

"You can stay with us," she says. "Don't worry about a thing. I'll help you cover rent, and you can pay me back whenever you're working again."

"I appreciate that, but it's not necessary. I can apply for a union loan."

"I'm better than that. No application needed." She leans toward me. "Hey, you don't have to do everything by yourself anymore. You have family. Me, Eli, Theo."

My eyes well. "I don't want to impose. You just had Theo. You're not working—"

"The bakery's still doing well without me. Don't give it another thought."

The teakettle whistles, and she goes to prepare our tea. I'm happy to stay with Jenna longer. I adore Theo, and I know I'm a big help to her.

She glances at me over her shoulder. "And now you'll have time to work on your screenplay with no distractions."

Eli appears in the kitchen with Theo, who's fussing. Now there's a major distraction, but I don't mind. I smile widely, looking at my nephew. He's everything good about the world. Pure love. This writers' strike is a gift of time to stay connected to him.

Eli goes over to Jenna. "All right, he's changed. Time for a car ride."

Jenna kisses Eli and then Theo. "Guess what? Eve's staying with us longer. Her writers' union just went on strike."

"Happy to have your help," Eli says enthusiastically. "I mean, have you visit."

I laugh. "I'm sure the free babysitting sweetens the deal."

He smiles. "Hard to believe it takes three adults to handle one little baby." He gets serious. "It means a lot to me and Jenna to have you here."

"Me too," I say.

He nods once and heads toward the garage with Theo.

Jenna brings over two cups of tea in pink-patterned china teacups. My sister is surprisingly domestic considering she used to work in IT running complicated computer systems. Maybe that was Mom's influence on her. Dad and I muddled by with takeout and lots of pasta. I did most of the household chores and not very well.

I take a sip of tea.

"So what did you think of Dr. Russo?" she asks, and I nearly spew my tea. I choke on it instead.

She stares at me. "Are you okay?"

I cough. "Yeah, it just went down the wrong pipe."

"Oh, I was afraid you got off on the wrong foot with Dr. Russo."

"No," I manage, still coughing a little. I decide not to share about my night with Dominic and my decision to keep my distance. I don't want her to worry about any issues with me taking over at the Fall Harvest Festival tomorrow in her place.

"Dominic," she says. "I guess at this point I can call him by his name since I volunteer with him so much. He's single, you know."

I put on my best game face, pleasantly neutral. "Audrey pointed that out."

She looks to the ceiling. "She said they went out for drinks, but nothing came of it. No surprise. Her heart's still with a clueless man whose name rhymes with Moo Mobinson."

I laugh. "Drew Robinson?" That's Eli's oldest brother.

"Who else? Something happened between the two of them, and she's not telling. So annoying. I'm her lifelong friend. She's always called me an honorary sister. She's an only child, you know, so that's a big deal. And still, she won't dish the details."

I lift one shoulder in a shrug. "Maybe there aren't any details. Maybe nothing happened at all with Drew, and she's embarrassed people keep asking about it."

She sips her tea. "No, I'm pretty sure something happened. She has this tell. She twirls her hair when she's lying, even a little white lie, and that hair twirl comes out almost every time Drew's name comes up." She holds up a finger. "Same thing when she mentioned going out with Dominic."

"He mentioned they were just friends."

"To you? Interesting. Maybe he said that because he wants to ask you out."

I shake my head. "What's the point? I'm leaving soon."

"You don't know that. You could be here three months. A lot can happen in three months. I proposed to Eli one day shy of the three-month mark of our spectacular relationship."

"Oh, so now it's spectacular. At the time you thought it was a roller coaster. You broke up multiple times."

"Because I was scared. He stuck it out long enough to sneak into my heart. I worry you're just like me, except worse because you purposely choose to stay single. I was unconsciously ruining relationships."

I laugh. "Right. That's so much better."

She gives me a sly look. "Dominic's divorced too."

"Moving on."

"I'm just saying, you have stuff in common."

"Lots of people have divorce in common. That doesn't mean they should get together."

"Okay. You're right. But he's gorgeous, isn't he?"

"I didn't notice," I say primly.

She gives my arm a playful smack, and we crack up.

Dominic

The Fall Harvest Festival is on a large piece of preserved grassy land with tall shade trees next to the Presbyterian church. It's a crisp fall day in a beautiful setting, and I'd like to enjoy that, but I can't because I'm annoyed that Eve's late. I had to do all the setup myself—the tent, the table and chairs, the raffle stuff, the meet-the-stray animal area, and the crates of adoptable animals. Jenna would've been here.

I'm sitting with PJ, a senior citizen black and white Boston terrier, on my lap. He's like my dog mascot since no one ever wants to adopt him. I'm not sure if it's because he's old or because he looks perpetually annoyed and above it all. He can't help that with his squashed-in face, jowls, and tired eyes. People don't get excited over him like the other dogs. Hell, he doesn't even get excited over me, and I spend the most time with him. I love him anyway.

The festival is in full swing with kids running around and parents chasing after them when Eve finally shows up to volunteer.

"Isn't this a perfect fall day?" she asks as she approaches. "I miss the fall foliage in LA. Look at those perfect white fluffy clouds."

I grumble an agreement. Seeing her in a short yellow dress that swings around her legs when she walks isn't helping my mood. Why do I want her so much? She pushes me away, refuses to give me her number, and shows up late for volunteering. Last night she left early. Of course, that kiss might've had something to do with it.

"Nice scrubs," she says, joining me at the table.

"It helps when you're handling animals."

"And who's this cutie?" She holds out her hand for PJ to sniff. His pointy ears turn toward her. He opens his eyes and gives her one of his classic haughty looks.

"This is PJ."

"Aww, aren't you adorable?" she asks and pets him behind the ears. He allows it, closing his eyes. When she stops, he makes a snuffling sound and nudges her hand for more. Wow. PJ actually likes her. He doesn't like anyone enough to seek out affection, except me, but I'm constantly giving him treats. She's not even holding a treat.

She scoops him up and settles him in her lap. "PJ, I'm sure you'll draw a crowd to enter the raffle and check out all these other cuties." She glances back at the cats and two other small dogs. Then she leans close to him and says, "You're the cutest, though."

He leans back against her chest and sighs.

My heart cracks open. I can't even stay mad at her when she's so great with animals. She's sexy catnip.

No, don't let her off the hook. She was supposed to be helping.

"Sorry I was late," she says. "Jenna had a baby emergency. The umbilical cord fell off earlier than she thought it would, and there was blood. She wanted to rush Theo to the emergency room, and she and Eli were arguing over what to do. Eli was adamant about not going to the hospital because Theo's so young and there's a lot of germs there. So while they were freaking out, the baby started howling, and that just made it worse because Jenna thought he was in pain."

"So did they go to the ER?"

"Luckily, I kept my cool and looked it up on the internet. Turns out bleeding is normal after the umbilical cord falls off. And it can happen within one to three weeks. It's been a week now. I told them that and then took Theo and calmed him down while Jenna broke down in sobs. The new-mom hormones are rough."

Guess that's a valid excuse. "I thought you flaked on setting up stuff."

"Big strong guy like you can handle setup, right?" She looks around. "There's tons of people here. I'm sure you could've had someone help you if it was a two-person job."

The place is overrun with volunteers, as well as families enjoying the day. That's not the point. Part of why I'm mad is because I want her, and I don't *want* to want her.

A family approaches with a young red-haired girl with braids. "Can I pet your dog?" she asks Eve.

"Sure can," Eve says. "Just touch him really gently right here behind his ear."

"His ears are triangles," the girl says.

"They are," Eve says. "I think it helps him hear extra good."

Eve's good with animals and kids too. Not that it matters. She's leaving tomorrow and doesn't want ties. Just proves my point—a good woman you can count on for the long haul doesn't exist.

For once, I hate to be right.

I introduce myself to the parents and tell them about our raffle for gift cards to Summerdale Sweets. While they're filling out some raffle tickets, I do my standard spiel about the animals, gesturing toward the crates.

"Behind me are adoptable cats and dogs looking for a good home. Let me know if you'd like to visit with one of them, and I'm happy to take them out of their crate. There's a play area you can sit in with them over there." I gesture over my shoulder to the portable enclosure I use both at the shelter and in town. "PJ here is also for adoption, if you don't mind an older dog."

PJ eyes them with his usual haughty look. They nod but don't pet him. Then they hurry their daughter away.

"I'd take PJ if I could," Eve says.

"You would?"

She pets him and kisses the top of his head. I've never been jealous of a dog before. "Yeah, I like his funny expressions, and he's real mellow."

"That's because he's old. He wouldn't do well on a flight because of his short muzzle, so you can't take him with you. Not good for his breathing. It's too bad, though, because no one has wanted to adopt him in two years."

"I can't anyway. My apartment doesn't allow pets. Why don't you adopt him?"

"In a way I have. He always hangs around in the waiting room or in my office."

"But you don't take him home with you."

"I'm still hoping he'll find a forever home."

"I have a feeling you're it for him."

I tip PJ's face up. "Is that true? Am I stuck with you?"

She cuddles him closer. "He's stuck with you. You'd be lucky to have him."

PJ lifts his brows in an expression that says *are you done with this nonsense?*

"Maybe I will," I say.

"There's a good vet."

I let out a breath. "I thought this might be awkward after—"

"I'm not leaving tomorrow."

My brows shoot up in surprise. "You're not?"

She keeps her eyes on PJ, petting him gently. "Nope. The writers' union went on strike. Jenna needs me, so I'm staying."

A ray of hope has me sitting up straighter. "For how long?"

"No idea. A week, a month? I hope not too long. I'm not getting paid."

I lean close. "Bright side is you'll get more time with PJ here."

Her lips quirk, and she finally meets my eyes. "And my nephew."

"Sounds like there's no reason we can't spend more time together."

"Dominic, I'm going back to LA eventually."

"We can keep it casual."

She gives me a sexy smile. "Can I get that in writing?"

6

I force a smile back. Not desperate here, even if she does have me hooked more than I'd ever admit. "I own my practice and recently built the animal shelter. I'm rooted here." *In more than just my business.* "I'm definitely not into a relationship, especially long distance."

She gives me a sideways look. "Jenna told me you're divorced."

I look away, not wanting to get into that mess. Drama at the time, and now that Lexi's back in my life, fresh drama during my every-other-Sunday visits at her apartment in the city. I can't talk about it without getting pissed off. Luckily, just then an older couple approaches, and I don't have to answer any questions. I know them—Mr. and Mrs. Chesterman. I had to put their elderly cat to sleep after a long bout with cancer. By far the most difficult part of my job.

I show them to a mother-daughter calico cat pair I recently took in, and thankfully they fall in love with them. Nothing is better than finding a good home for animals. I put the cats together in a large cardboard carrier I use at events.

"And you get five free raffle tickets for Summerdale Sweets gift cards," I tell them.

Eve holds up the tickets. I hand the carrier to Mr. Chesterman and join Eve at the table.

Mrs. Chesterman smiles at me. "If we win, we'll send them to you. Such a sweet young man." She turns to Eve. "He took wonderful care of our Oreo, and when the time came to say goodbye, he showed such compassion and sensitivity. I hope you appreciate what you've got with him."

"That's good to hear, but we're, uh, not together," Eve says.

"No?" she asks, looking between us. "Sure seems that way."

Mr. Chesterman nods. "You do look like a couple. Very well matched."

Eve shakes her head.

"She's just volunteering today," I say. "Thank you so much for adopting Dot and Myrtle. Feel free to rename them."

"Dot and Myrtle are perfect," Mrs. Chesterman says.

After they leave, Eve says to PJ, "Not as perfect as you."

I can't resist. "Have dinner with me tonight."

"Is that code for a booty call?"

"No."

She nudges my shoulder with hers. "Damn, I was hoping."

My lips curve up. This sounds promising. I pull my phone out. "So I finally get your number."

She takes my phone and types in her number. "When did you get your divorce?"

"Three years ago. And that's all I'll say about that."

"I'm divorced too. Jenna told me we had that in common."

She hands my phone back. "And we have matching knee scars."

"If I found you on a dating app and it said divorced, knee scar, not interested in a relationship, I would've been all over that."

She laughs, her pale blue eyes twinkling. "I bet."

∽

Eve

I'm a little on edge now that I've basically agreed to see Dominic again by giving him my number. I think we're on the same page with seeing each other casually, but there's always a chance of messy complications. I've spent an hour helping out at the tent with him, and I'm about to bolt, err, excuse myself for a much-needed break. Just as I'm about to hand PJ over to Dominic, Audrey appears at the table.

"Hi, guys." She's not dressed in her usual modest-style outfit of a buttoned-up blouse and tailored pants. Today she's wearing a floral blouse with a V-neck that shows some cleavage with tight jeans and black heeled ankle boots. She wore makeup too—pink lips and heavy emphasis around her pretty blue eyes. It looks like she's going on a date.

She glances at me briefly before turning to Dominic. "Now that Jenna's busy with the baby, I thought I'd step in to volunteer with you. The animals too, of course." She laughs.

"That's great," Dominic says. "Eve will be in town longer since her union's on strike. Maybe the two of you could work together."

"Sure." She leans close to Dominic, smiling. "Cinder is doing well on the new food. I'm so glad we have a great vet in town."

"Great! I think her energy will start improving in a few more weeks with the vitamin B injections."

"You're like a cat whisperer," she says admiringly.

He grins, his eyes sparkling. "Dog whisperer too. Occasionally I tweet to a bird."

She laughs. "You're so funny."

I tense, suddenly irritated. Am I jealous or is it more envious? They're so relaxed and easy with each other like real friends. I've never had a friendship with a guy. Is that why all my relationships end horribly? Is friendship a prerequisite to having a successful relationship? Are Audrey and Dominic at the start of their own relationship?

Maybe I'm the third wheel. My ribs squeeze tight, and I'm suddenly finding it hard to take a deep breath.

I stand and hand PJ to Dominic. "Audrey, could you take my spot? I'm going to take a walk to stretch my legs."

"I'd be happy to," she says, hurrying around the table to take my place.

"You're coming back, right?" Dominic asks me.

"Yes. Unless you don't need me."

"PJ will miss you too much," he says, holding up PJ, who gives me a slow blink.

"Uh-huh."

I go for a walk around the fairgrounds, looking for a familiar face. There's a lot of new families in town since the school district is so good. Jenna told me the high school earned a blue-ribbon award recently for being the best in the state. Guess that means the elementary and middle schools are also above average. I was only here for part of elementary school, so I wouldn't know.

In the church parking lot, there're kiddie games set up, as well as food tents for The Horseman Inn and Summerdale Sweets. I stop by the Summerdale Sweets tent, where Jenna's best friend from way back, Sydney, is working, expertly handling a pack of teenaged boys buying brownies and cookies. Her auburn hair is up in a high ponytail, and she's wearing an official pink Summerdale Sweets T-shirt. Behind her, a baby sleeps in her stroller with the shade pulled down. I can just see her pink leather booties with white daisies peeking out.

After the boys leave, I step forward. "Hi, Sydney, how's it going here?"

"Hey, Eve!" She leans across the table and hugs me. "How're you doing?"

"Good. I'm stepping in for Jenna over at the animal tent."

"How's she doing?"

"Tired. She said you were battling morning sickness, but you look great."

She scowls. "She wasn't supposed to say anything."

"Oops! Sorry. I won't tell anyone."

"It's just that it's early days. Anyway, I'm okay at the

moment. I had some baguette earlier, which helps settle my stomach."

An older couple approaches and orders a bag of cookies to share.

"Seems like you're pretty busy," I say, stepping to the side.

"Yeah, and there's a lot of people at Jenna's shop too. Her assistant's been scrambling. I let Jenna know business is good."

"I could step in to help, here or there, either one."

"No, you go ahead back to your station. I know Dominic depends on Jenna's help a lot."

I cock my head. "Wouldn't she normally be here at her tent?"

She looks over my shoulder. "Can I help you?"

I glance back at a trio of young girls clutching money. Why am I at Dominic's tent volunteering if Jenna is normally here at her tent? Is Jenna setting me up with Dominic? It would've been nice if she'd told me instead of doing this behind my back.

I wait until Sydney helps the girls with their treats before pressing her for more information. "Is Jenna setting me up with Dominic?"

She gestures me closer. "You didn't hear this from me. Jenna asked me and Audrey to run her tent, but then Audrey wanted to help with the animals. We're not sure how much is due to Dominic or the animals."

"So why was I also assigned to Dominic?"

"Jenna and I thought another pretty woman volunteering would make Audrey try harder to get his attention if that's what she's after. She's way too subtle. Guys need clear signals."

"So I was bait."

She waves that away. "No, no, not bait. Just a little enticement to get Audrey to make a move. Eve, she's thirty-one, and she's been wanting to settle down with a husband and child of her own for longer than any of us. We didn't think it would hurt anything since you're just visiting."

She gestures over to The Horseman Inn tent. "My staff has it under control. And my husband—that's the handsome devil over there in the white apron with the thick dark hair and killer bod—is close by to take Quinn if I need him to. He's got a way with our daughter. Guess it helps that he has three younger sisters." She spreads her arms wide. "All good here."

I glance back at the animal tent, where Audrey looks entranced by whatever Dominic's saying. My jaw clenches. I don't know exactly what the situation is over there; I just know I don't belong. "Okay, see you later."

"Sure thing."

I head back to the tent. I'm just going to let them know I'm leaving. I'll hang with baby Theo and let Jenna know that from now on, I want to be in on any man schemes involving me. I'm not real happy about being manipulated like that.

I'm halfway to the table when I'm joined by an elderly woman with short white hair and sharp brown eyes. It's Mrs. Joan Ellis, Jenna's scary third-grade teacher. I never had her for class because I left town before I was old enough. A fact I was happy about. Kids regularly came home in tears from her class and weighed down with homework.

"Eve Larsen, good to see you in town again."

"Hi, Mrs. Ellis, good to see you too."

"How're your sister and the baby doing?"

"Theo. They're both great."

"Do you have a picture?"

"Of course." I stop and pull my phone from my purse to show her.

She puts a hand to her chest. "He's precious. You know I'm the one who got Jenna and Eli together."

That's not how I heard it. I put my phone away. "Is that right?"

She starts walking toward the animal tent with a slight limp due to a bad hip. "I've gotten countless single people together. In fact, I'm running out of singles here in town."

Jenna mentioned that Mrs. Ellis thinks of herself as Cupid,

while everyone else secretly calls her the General for her stern nature. Though I have to admit at eighty-something (or is it ninety?), she seems to have mellowed from her school-teaching days.

I gesture toward the tent where Dominic and Audrey are talking to a young family. "There's a couple of singles right there."

"Pshaw. They don't need my help. Dominic asked her out for drinks months ago. Don't they look good together?"

"I don't think they're actually together."

She lets out a long-suffering sigh. "This is why single people need me so much. They can't close the deal with all the hubbub over not labeling a relationship, not wanting to be the first to commit. In my day, you had a formal courtship, and a few months later, you knew if you were heading for marriage or breaking up. Much simpler."

We reach the tent, and sweet Cupid transforms to the General right before my eyes.

"Audrey, what is going on with you?" Mrs. Ellis barks.

Audrey jumps. "General Joan!" She slaps a hand over her mouth. "Sorry!"

General Joan lets out a cackling laugh. "You think I didn't know you girls called me that behind my back? I consider it an honor. The general is the highest in the chain of command."

Audrey salutes her.

"Don't get fresh, young lady," the General snaps.

"Sorry," Audrey says, instantly contrite.

"Are you two together?" the General asks, pointing at Dominic and Audrey.

"No," Audrey says, her cheeks flushing pink.

"We're just friends," Dominic says, locking eyes with me.

The General takes a hard look at me before turning back to them. "Audrey, he's old enough to settle down, a veteran, and a man who owns his own business. Make your move, girl!"

Audrey smooths her hair. "Mrs. Ellis, he takes good care

of my cat, and I so appreciate that. Cinder hasn't been doing so well."

I point vaguely behind me. "I was about to get back to Jenna and the baby. Looks like you have this under control."

Mrs. Ellis waves wildly across the way. "Yoo-hoo! Drew! Come here."

Drew Robinson, Eli's oldest brother, walks over wearing his white karate uniform with a black belt. We met once before at Jenna's wedding, and he gave me the briefest of hellos, his eyes scanning the room at the same time like he was on guard. Probably because he used to be a soldier, former Army Ranger. There's something lethal looking about him, the way his gaze narrows in on his target, which isn't Mrs. Ellis. It's Audrey.

He stops next to Mrs. Ellis, the hard angles of his face not softened at all by his longish dark hair and scruffy jaw. A near opposite to his clean-shaven, cheerful brother Eli. "Hi, Mrs. Ellis. What can I help you with?" His gaze drifts back to Audrey and then lands on Dominic with a hard stare.

Mrs. Ellis smacks his arm to get his attention. "I wanted to reintroduce you to Eve Larsen, Jenna's younger sister. You probably don't remember her from when she lived in town, it was so long ago."

Drew seems to notice me for the first time, doing a quick scan of my features. When his brown eyes meet mine, his are guarded, hiding pain. I know that look. I had it for years and years. A wounded soul.

"We've met," he says gruffly.

"Yup, at Jenna's wedding. Very briefly. It was a busy day."

General Joan turns to me. "You left town when you were still very young. How old are you now?"

And how old are you, nosy woman? "Twenty-nine."

She gestures between me and Drew. "Drew here is seven years older than you. Single, and a veteran who owns his own business. Like this guy—" she gestures to Dominic "—except available."

"I'm available," Dominic protests.

Drew shifts uncomfortably and glances at Audrey.

I cough to cover up a laugh. "Those are very nice credentials."

The General nods once, looking pleased. "Seeing as how Drew is the very last single man I haven't managed to match yet, I think you two should go out for a get-to-know-you drink."

Audrey stares at the ground while Drew stares at her.

Unsure how to respond without insulting either the General or Drew, I just stand there. He is my brother-in-law, after all. I have to see him at family functions.

General Joan pokes Drew in the shoulder. "How about making Eve feel welcome in town?"

He turns to me. "Sure." He pulls a business card from his pocket. "Stop by my dojo for a free karate lesson on Wednesday at seven o'clock."

The General looks to the sky.

I take his card. "I've always wanted to learn self-defense." And this could really help with an idea I've been noodling with for an action-adventure movie with a female martial arts expert.

Drew flashes a smile that takes him from menacing to almost...nice. "I look forward to seeing you there, Eve. I need to get back to our tent. Just took a quick break to get me and Caleb some bottled water. We have more demos in the afternoon if you want to check it out."

"I have to get back to Jenna."

"Too bad," he says, sounding like he really means it.

What a nice guy. Well, he is Eli's brother.

The General walks away, muttering to herself about knuckleheads.

I wave to Dominic and Audrey. "Have fun, guys. Hope you find many happy homes for the animals."

"Are you really taking a karate class with him?" Dominic asks me tightly.

"I'm in that karate class too," Audrey says brightly. "So I guess I'll see you there."

Dominic's eyes bore into mine. "Maybe I'll be there too."

"Oh, you should come," Audrey says to him. "It's a great class."

I back away. "Sounds like a party. Bye."

I head to my car, unsure what just happened back there. Some very confusing vibes.

It's not until I reach my car that it hits me—General Joan was playing one guy off the other for Audrey's benefit to get Audrey and Drew together. Pretty sure. Or was it for Audrey and Dominic? The General doesn't know me well enough to play matchmaker. Besides, everyone knows I'm just visiting Summerdale.

7

When I get back to Jenna's place, I find her on the sofa, nursing Theo. I was still a little miffed she manipulated the situation to put me at Dominic's tent without letting me in on the plan, but now that I see her in a bulky, stained nursing shirt and fleece pants with my precious nephew in her arms, it's hard to stay mad. She's doing her best in this new messy exhausting phase of her life.

"How'd it go?" she whispers.

"I thought we weren't whispering around the baby."

"He's against my chest. I don't want to startle him and get a bite."

I wince and take a seat next to her. "Two things: I accidentally mentioned Sydney's pregnancy to her."

"Oops."

"Yeah, and second, she told me that the two of you put me at Dominic's table just to get Audrey to make her move. I'd appreciate a heads-up the next time you're using me in a guy situation."

"Sorry. You're right. We were thinking more about Audrey and getting her on track. Dominic's a nice guy, so I thought you'd get along fine, and it wouldn't make a difference to you either way."

"Yeah, about that."

She takes Theo off her breast, adjusts her shirt, and puts him upright against her chest, patting his back to burp him. "What? Did Audrey say something to you?"

"Like what?"

She narrows her eyes, trying to look menacing. "Like, get lost, this man is mine."

I lift my brows. "Sweet librarian Audrey?"

"I know, I know, but she's been feeling left out with all of us having babies when she's the one who wanted kids for so long. I thought maybe she got more aggressive on her man hunt."

I shake my head. "I don't think she would know how. It's about Dominic."

"You have a problem with Dominic? Everyone in town loves him."

"I had a fling with him in LA."

"What!"

Theo bursts into tears, and she stands, soothing him as she paces back and forth, sending me a dark look. He calms down a few moments later and finally lets out a burp, settling against her.

She carefully sits next to me again, keeping him against her chest. "Okay, how am I just now hearing about this?" Her eyes widen. "Oh my God, he's the *four orgasms in a night* fling, isn't he?"

"Yup."

She stares at me, mouth agape. "You must've been shocked when you saw him at the fundraiser. And today too! How could you not say anything?"

"I didn't want you to feel bad about asking me to step in to volunteer in your place, so I told myself it was fine. Nothing was going to happen anyway. I'd just play it real casual and chill."

She looks at me expectantly, waiting for the rest of the story.

"And then I kissed him."

Her jaw drops.

"I know. That was before I knew I was going to be in town for a while, and today we were kind of…flirty, so I gave him my number."

"Ooh, sounds serious," she says in a mocking tone. "You gave him your number."

"The moment I did, I started having second thoughts, and then here comes Audrey. The two of them seemed so comfortable together. I felt like a third wheel, so I left."

Jenna cocks her head. "Comfortable? No sizzling chemistry?"

"It's hard to tell with her." Though now that I'm not in the throes of envy or whatever that was watching the two of them together, Dominic seemed warm and kind toward her not flirty. Is it selfish that I don't want Dominic to be with Audrey? It's not like Dominic and I have a future.

I nudge her shoulder. "Oh! And then General Joan came along and told Audrey to step up her game with Dominic. Then the General called Drew Robinson over and told him to ask *me* out."

Her eyes widen. "She's playing a high-level game there. The woman is ninety and doesn't miss a thing."

"I thought so too. She's playing the two guys off each other to get Audrey with Drew." *Hopefully.*

"Or she wants Audrey with Dominic, but where do you fit in?"

"I think I'm just part of the strategy. She knows I live in LA, right?"

"Yeah. She's a crafty one, though. It's hard to know her true intent."

"Anyway, Drew invited me to a free karate class on Wednesday that Audrey also goes to, and Dominic said he'd be there too."

She twists her lips to the side, thinking for a moment. "You know, Audrey has had a thing for Drew forever, but he treats her like his best friend's little sister. She's been in that karate class for months. She's a yellow belt going for whatever color's next. Hard-core dedication, and Drew treats her just like every other student."

"So will me being there help or hurt her chances with him?"

"Are you interested in Drew?"

"Only for screenplay purposes. I've got this idea for a martial arts heroine with a dark past. Maybe he could give me some insight just by being him."

"Then I don't see how it can hurt her. Maybe Audrey will have two men fighting over her."

My gut twists into a knot. Drew and Dominic in a battle for Audrey's heart. I don't have a claim on Dominic. I'm a temporary distraction to his life here.

She smiles. "This is her big moment. Finally, she gets to be adored."

I stroke Theo's back. "Right. Good for her."

"I've got to get to this class!"

$\approx$

That night Jenna's wound tight over our parents' upcoming visit. She downed six cookies and then started running up and down the stairs, afraid to give Theo a sugar rush through her milk that would have him up all night. I finally told her to take a nap while I watch the baby.

Our parents will be here any moment. Eli's finishing up his shift at work.

"What do you think, Theo?" I ask him as I take him on a tour of the downstairs area—living room, dining room, kitchen, and back. "Are you ready to meet your grandparents?" Unfortunately, Eli's parents are both deceased, so these are Theo's only grandparents. My parents recently both turned fifty. They had us young. Mom dropped out of college her freshman year to have Jenna, and Dad did too to get a full-time job. Their parents cut them off for the accidental pregnancy. It couldn't have been easy for them.

It helps me to stay in a forgiving mood by taking their

perspective. No one is all good or all bad. I'm closer to Dad since I lived with him. He encouraged my writing, and when my best and only friend betrayed me in high school, Dad and I spent a lot of time together watching movies. It's probably what ultimately made me want to get into screenwriting.

"Things get complicated when you get older," I tell Theo. "Enjoy this time while you can."

He makes a gurgling sound. I pat him on the back in case he needs to burp. "You get it."

I hear a car pull into the driveway and peek out the front window. "They're here, and it's just us. I hate to wake your mama."

I go to the front door and open it in advance of their knock. "Hi!" I call.

Mom hurries over. "Is that him?"

"No, I'm holding a random baby."

She shoots me a look that says she's not amused. "Nice to see you, Eve. You look well." My whole family are tall, lean blondes. Dad's blond hair is turning white in places, and his cheeks are rounder than the rest of ours, making him look friendly and approachable. Mom colors her hair, so there's no white. Jenna and I mostly take after her in looks.

"Evie!" Dad says jovially. "It's been too long. Why'd you have to move to LA?"

"Because that's where all the TV jobs are."

"Right."

I turn and head for the sofa. Mom sits next to me while Dad just stands off to the side, looking around.

"Can I hold him?" Mom asks.

"Of course." I hand Theo over.

She coos at him, holding him close to her chest. Then she shifts, supporting his head with one hand as she gazes at him in total adoration.

I look away, my leg bouncing up and down. I wonder if she held me and Jenna like that. I don't really know. I have no pictures of that time since I lived with Dad, and Mom basically abandoned me when she gave up custody. Agitated, I do a mental scan of my body, deliberately relaxing every tense muscle from my jaw all the way down to my toes. I learned that in therapy. Every time I think I've moved past the hurt, something reminds me of it. Maybe that's why it's easier to live three thousand miles away. No reminders.

I glance at Dad standing stiffly. "Why don't you have a seat?"

He shoves his hands in his pockets. "Where's Jenna and Eli?"

"Eli's on his way home from work. Jenna's upstairs. I'll go get her."

I hurry up the steps. As much as I feel bad waking Jenna, I don't want to face our parents alone. It's just weird that they're a couple now after their tumultuous divorce. And then there was the botched wedding, where Mom ran away, and now they live together without the official marriage certificate. Maybe some people are meant to be together even though they don't get it right the first time. It's the only explanation besides our parents being nuts. I'd like to give them the benefit of the doubt.

When I get to Jenna's bedroom, she's already awake, staring at the ceiling.

"Hi, they're here."

She blows out a long breath. "I know. I'm just taking a few calming breaths before I go down."

"Don't worry. Theo's a great buffer. Mom's holding him, and she's already in love."

She sits up. "Hmm, maybe this'll make every family dinner easier, right? It's all about the grandchild."

"Possibly."

She swings her legs to the side of the bed and sits there for a moment. "Let's go with that best-case scenario. I don't like how stressed I get every time I see them."

"That's what therapy is for. And good boundaries."

"Ha. Seems I found an easier solution. Having a kid."

"Now why didn't I think of that?"

She laughs and leads the way downstairs. When we get

there, Dad's holding Theo while Mom stands next to him, talking to Theo in a singsong voice. "That's your grandpop. Yes, it is. What a beautiful little boy you are!"

"Hi, Mom. Hi, Dad," Jenna says. "Looks like you met Theo."

Mom hugs Jenna. "Oh, Jenna, he's just perfect. I'm so happy for you and Eli."

"Thanks."

"Can I get anyone anything?" I ask.

"Some water would be great," Mom says.

"Me too," Jenna says.

"I'm okay," Dad says.

I head to the kitchen as the three of them get settled on the sofa. My phone chimes with a text, and I pull it from my back jeans pocket.

Dominic: *How's tonight for dinner?*

A zing of excitement rushes through me. It seems like nothing happened with Audrey after I left the Fall Harvest Festival earlier today. Still, I'm leaving. And part of me fears this thing between us could turn into a relationship, which scares the crap out of me because it obviously can't work out with the long distance, and none of my relationships ever work out.

Deep breath.

Me: *I think it's best if we're just friends.* I immediately delete that. I don't want to be friends. I need distance.

Me: *I'm really busy with the baby and family stuff.*

No response.

I put my phone away, my throat tight. I did the right thing. I get two glasses of water and head back to the family room, handing them over. Just then Eli arrives. My parents light up at his arrival and make more of a fuss over Eli than they did Jenna.

"Congratulations!" Dad says, shaking his hand and patting his back at the same time in a man hug.

"Yes, congratulations!" Mom says. "He looks just like you. Spitting image."

Eli's chest puffs out. "Thanks, but I'm sure he's got a little of Jenna in him too."

"Maybe around the eyes," Mom says. "But mostly he looks like a Robinson."

Eli goes to Jenna and kisses her cheek. "How're you?"

"Good," she says tightly. "We should order dinner. Can you pick it up at The Horseman?"

"Absolutely."

A few minutes later, Eli calls in our order and sets the dining room table for us. It's so nice to see a hands-on man who just jumps in to help where needed. I don't know if he came that way or if Jenna trained him right, but it's awesome. Dad depended on me to do stuff around the house even from a young age.

Our visit goes much more smoothly than normal. It's all down to baby magic. Mom and Dad spend the whole time looking at Theo, talking to him, holding him, showing him a rattle. Jenna and I barely need to say a word. In fact, I feel like we could leave and our parents wouldn't notice.

Mom holds the baby during dinner, eating with one hand. She hasn't wanted to let go of him. "I missed holding a baby," she tells us. "I loved every moment of you girls' babyhood. You were both so cute and sweet." She sniffs Theo's head. "There's nothing like that new-baby smell."

"It's a magical time," Dad says.

"I was just thinking there was some baby magic around here," I say. "Look at how well we're all getting along."

Mom lifts her brows at me.

Dad clears his throat. "It's good to have the family all together again."

They go back to admiring the baby while we finish up dinner. Eli and I make quick work of the dishes and clearing the take-out containers. When we get back to the dining room, there's tension in the air.

Jenna sends me a pointed look. "Mom wants to talk to us."

My gaze snaps to Mom, who looks serious, and then to Dad, who looks somber.

Jenna holds her arms out for Theo, and Mom hands him over. Jenna cuddles him close like he's a baby defense barrier against whatever our parents have to say. I really hope it's not that they're getting married again.

"Well, girls, there's no easy way to say this." Mom takes a deep breath. "I have breast cancer, and I'm scheduled for a mastectomy in three weeks."

My stomach drops. *Mommy.*

"Oh, Mom," Jenna says softly.

"I'm so sorry," I say, my throat closing. I guess I always thought there'd be time down the road to patch things up with Mom. The possibility of losing her makes me queasy. She's too young.

"Her prognosis is good," Dad says.

"Yes," Mom says. "Once I'm healed from surgery, I'll have radiation treatment. That should be the end of it. I just wanted you to know."

Jenna and I exchange a scared look.

Jenna's eyes well. "Mom, I can't lose you. You're Theo's only grandmother."

Mom scoots her chair closer and puts her arm around her. "You're not going to lose me. This is a blip. That's all."

"Anything I can do to help, just let me know," Eli says. "If you need a ride, groceries, or just want to see Theo, all you have to do is text or call."

"Thank you, Eli. We're so lucky to have you for a son-in-law," Mom says.

"Real lucky," Dad says.

"Can I hold him again?" Mom asks Jenna in a quivery voice.

Jenna hands Theo over and gives Mom a sideways hug around the baby.

Mom rubs Theo's back. "The doctor says I'll have to stay away from the baby during radiation treatment, so I just want to soak him in while I can. Apparently, I'm radioactive for a bit."

"Let's go to lunch," I blurt. "Let me know what day works for you next week."

Everyone stares at me, surprised. I'm a little surprised myself. I haven't spent any time alone with Mom since I was a little girl.

"Well, there's my silver lining," Mom says with a watery smile.

I sniffle, my eyes hot, my throat tight. Dad puts his arm around me, and I lean against his shoulder, accepting the comfort gratefully. It seems my family is finally pulling together.

I let out a breath that feels very much like relief.

Early Monday morning I run a quick errand for Jenna, picking up bread and bananas at the local grocery store, and on the way home I spot a small dog on the side of the road, lying on its side. Was it hit by a car?

I pull over and get out of the car. It's a black and tan York-shire terrier. It's so still. Is it dead?

I creep closer, and the dog blinks. Oh, thank God. "Hi," I say softly. "What happened?" It's not wearing a collar. "Did you hurt yourself?"

The dog tries to stand and then collapses with a cry. My heart lurches. I crouch next to him and gently stroke behind his ears. "It's okay. I'll help you."

I pull my phone from my purse and glance at the time. Seven a.m. We get up early at Jenna's house thanks to Theo. I hope Dominic's awake.

I tap on his number and wait. The dog's just lying there, blinking.

"Hello." His voice sounds rough.

"Hi, it's Eve. I'm on Peaceable Lane, not far from the Summerdale Mart. There's an injured dog collapsed on the side of the road. Can you take a look at him?"

"Five minutes. Don't move him."

"Thank you!" He already hung up. I turn to the dog. "Someone's going to help you feel better soon." I gently stroke his head. "You're okay, sweet doggie." He closes his eyes. Alarmed, I check that he's still breathing. Yes, his rib cage is rising and falling.

I send a quick text to Jenna that I'll be late. The minutes tick by slowly as I keep talking to the dog in a soothing voice, stroking his head gently.

Finally, a white van pulls up behind us. The side reads Summerdale Animal Hospital. Dominic steps out of the van, wearing scrubs and carrying a black duffel bag.

"What do we have here?" he asks, unzipping the duffel bag. He pulls latex gloves on before putting a stethoscope around his neck and pulling out a small light.

I watch as he gently examines the dog, checking his eye response to the light and listening to his heart.

"I just found him here," I say. "He tried to stand and collapsed."

He gently moves his legs, and the dog remains silent. "Legs seem fine. Okay, I'm just going to gently lift you." The dog cries out as he's lifted. Dominic peers at his side, and I do too. There's an open wound with blood oozing. Bile rises in my throat. Dominic gently sets him down on his uninjured side.

"Something took a bite out of you," Dominic says to the dog, pulling gauze and sterile pads from his bag. "You must be a feisty one to get away." He starts bandaging the wound. "Eve, grab the small carrier from the back of the van. It's unlocked."

I hurry over to the back of the van, where there's a variety of empty animal carriers secured in the van. I undo the safety belt around a small one. There's a fleece blanket inside it. What a nice touch for the animals.

When I return, the dog has white gauze wrapped securely around his middle. Dominic efficiently unclips the top of the plastic carrier, slowly and gently lifts the dog, who cries again, and settles him on the blanket. He puts the carrier top back on, locks it securely in place, and strides back to the van.

I follow him. "What could've bit him?"

"I'm guessing a coyote." He secures the carrier in the back while he talks. "They roam the area, and tiny dogs are a meal for them."

He shuts the van door.

"Will he survive?" I ask over the lump in my throat.

"I'll do my best. The rest is up to him."

Then he gets in the driver's seat and takes off.

I run a hand through my hair. It's the first time I've seen Dominic in action as Dr. Russo. He was incredible—gentle, skilled, compassionate. If anyone could heal this dog, it's him.

8

I'm just finishing lunch with Jenna when I get a text from Dominic that says, *He's a fighter. I think he's going to make it.* There's a picture too of the Yorkshire terrier from this morning, awake and resting on a soft blanket, a bandage wrapped around his middle. He has an IV too.

"Oh, thank God."

"What is it?" Jenna asks.

I show her the picture. "Dominic says he thinks the dog will be okay."

"Of course he will. Didn't I tell you we have the best veterinarian?"

I text back. *Great news! I'm so glad you could be there for him.*

Dominic: *Of course. That's what I do.*

A man who shows up when needed. It wasn't for me, it was for a dog, but it means something. My heart warms toward him.

I text back. *Can I see him?*

Dominic: *Sure.*

I turn to Jenna. "Do you mind if I stop by the animal hospital to see the dog?"

She gives me a sly smile. "Just the dog?" At my dark look, she shoos me away. "Go. It's on Route 15." She gives me directions.

I nod and grab my purse. "I wonder if the dog is a stray."

"If he is, he's in the right place. Dominic's animal shelter is state of the art."

I bite back a smile, almost afraid to feel too much where Dominic's concerned. Still, it's good to hear how well he cares for animals in need.

I pull into the driveway of the animal hospital and see three other cars there. I guess he has a busy practice.

I step into the waiting room with a woman waiting with her cat in a carrier and an older man with a Great Dane who lies patiently on the floor.

A brunette receptionist with a short bob of hair greets me cheerfully from behind the front counter. "Hello, can I help you?"

"Yes, I'm Eve. I'm here to see the Yorkshire terrier who was brought in this morning."

"Oh, yes, Dr. Russo said to go straight back to our recovery area. Just through that door on the right."

I push through a heavy swinging door, go down a hall-way, and find the recovery room, where Dominic's checking on the dog and talking to him at the same time. His voice is deep and soothing. "What a fighter you are, Henry. Your people are going to be so happy to see you." He takes a look at the IV level and seems satisfied.

"Hi."

Dominic whirls. "Hi. I didn't hear you come in."

I walk over to him, suddenly overwhelmed with affection for the man. I focus on Henry instead, stroking his silky head. His brown eyes are sleepy, probably from anesthesia. "So his name is Henry?"

"Yup. I found a microchip and contacted the owners. They'd been looking for him for two days. He slipped right out of his leash and collar when their five-year-old took him for a walk down the block. Henry took off after a squirrel through the woods, and the kid went home to get help."

"That's too young to walk a dog alone."

"I guess they figured it was safe on the sidewalk in front of their house."

I coo at Henry, coming down to his level on the table. "You're one lucky dog to have the best veterinarian rescue you."

"He's lucky you found him when you did." That deep voice scrapes against my insides.

I straighten, and our gazes lock, a tension shimmering in the air between us. I didn't realize how close we were standing. I can feel his heat. Every part of me wants to reach out to him.

My heart thuds against my rib cage as his blue eyes go half-mast, and his head slowly lowers toward mine.

A woman's voice calls out, "Dr. Russo, we have another emergency. Mrs. Rankin just pulled into the parking lot. Grover broke two of his teeth on a bone, and there's a lot of blood."

Dominic shakes his head. "I tell all my clients bones are too hard on a dog's teeth. Sorry, I gotta go. Stay as long as you'd like with Henry. He could use the company before his family gets here."

"Sure," I say, a little dazed from the near kiss.

He strides from the room, full of purpose, looking very much like a hero.

I meet Mom at Summerdale Pizza for lunch on Wednesday. I purposely chose this place because I thought it would be a quick lunch, and if things get too awkward, we can both bail. I know it sounds like I have one foot out the door, and that's because I do. I was always closer to Dad, and he's been there for me in a way she never was, even now as an adult. He's in love with her again, and I need to make peace with that. And between me and Mom before it's too late. What if she dies?

I bite my lower lip. It's hard not to worry. She's still my mom.

I look up just as she walks in, looking unsure of her welcome, her eyes meeting mine hopefully. I've never seen Mom look so vulnerable. She's always been bold and confident.

I wave at her from a booth.

She gives me a small smile and walks over. "What would you like? On me."

"Slice of pepperoni and—"

She smiles. "Lemonade." That was my favorite drink when we went to a restaurant as a kid.

"Actually, I stick to water now."

Her expression closes. "Of course."

She walks to the front counter to place the order, and I sit there sifting through possible conversational topics. What do we have in common besides our genes? Jenna, Dad, Theo, and Eli. I don't want to get into too heavy a conversation for our first lunch. This is just about starting to reconnect.

A short while later, she joins me with our pizza and drinks. She smiles tightly. "I'm so glad we could do this."

"Me too."

I hope you don't die.

Don't dwell on her diagnosis.

A mom with three little kids shows up, and the noise level rises tremendously. Besides them, there's just a few old men by the front of the shop talking over drinks.

We eat in silence, both of us eavesdropping on the little kids and their mom trying to keep order. She has two little boys, who can't stop touching each other—poking, hitting, shoving—and a toddler girl making a mess with the condiments.

"Keep your hands to yourself and finish your pizza," the mom hisses.

The older boy takes a bite of pizza and bumps into his brother's shoulder, making him spill his drink.

Mom and I look at each other, trying not to laugh. We go back to eating. I'm silently soaking in the dynamics of the family and their dialogue like I always do when I sit near interesting people. Mom's looking wistful, glancing frequently at the toddler girl.

They leave in a flurry of activity, napkins flying, as the mom hurries them out the door for their playdate at the park.

As soon as they leave, I say, "That looked exhausting."

"I was lucky. You and Jenna weren't like that. You got along well with each other, none of that pushing and shoving stuff. Jenna mostly followed the rules, and you were pretty quiet."

I force a pleasant expression. The last thing I want to talk about is my childhood. "How are you feeling?"

"Good. So what's new with you?"

"Well, the strike negotiations are at a standstill, I'm up at two a.m. every night with Theo's wailing, and tonight I'm taking a beginner karate class. I've always wanted to learn self-defense."

She brightens. "I'm so glad to hear it. I've worried about you living alone in LA. Dad says you're not allowed to have pets in your building, so no big dog to defend you."

"I didn't realize you worried about me." *I didn't know you thought of me.*

"Of course I do. I think about you every day, wondering how you're doing and if you're okay. Dad keeps me posted now, so that helps."

"Why didn't you just call or text me?"

She tucks her chin, drawing back. "I wasn't sure you'd want to hear from me."

Maybe that was true before, but I want to try now. "Mom—"

She leans across the table, whispering fiercely, "I'm so sorry for the distance between us since the divorce."

"Mom, you already apologized last Thanksgiving."

She holds up a palm. "Let me finish. It's my biggest regret. I wish I'd pushed harder to spend time with you when you were a kid, instead of letting you push me away. You were so angry when I tried to visit. And when I forced you to come home with me, you ran away. I didn't want a battle every time."

I was an angry, abandoned little girl. Mom and Jenna chose against me.

My lower lip quivers, and I bite down on it. "It's fine."

"No, it's not fine. I should've pushed past all that and forged a connection somehow. I abandoned my daughter. I'm not proud of it. Dad and I could've handled things a lot better. All I can say is I'm really, really sorry."

"You did abandon me," I say over the lump in my throat.

She reaches across the table to hold my hand. "I'm sorry. I never will again."

"What if you die, Mommy?" Tears leak out. I'm half embarrassed at my little-girl voice, and half terrified of losing her to cancer too soon. Next thing I know, she's in the booth next to me, her arms around me.

She kisses my hair. "You're not going to lose me now. This is a blip. I'm not going anywhere."

I cry for a few moments before pulling myself together, desperately wanting to believe that she'll stay in my life. I straighten up to look at her, surprised to see tears streaming silently down her face.

She grabs a napkin from the table and wipes her tears. "It's good that we're doing this."

I wipe my own tears with the back of my hand. "A cathartic lunch."

She laughs a little. "Yes. Let's do this every week, but with less crying."

"That sounds good to me."

She hugs me again for a very long time, and I let her.

I head to beginner adult karate class that night ready to kick ass. I feel stronger after my talk with Mom, and it'll be good to focus on something physical instead of all the angst over work, helplessness over Mom's disease, and thinking about

Dominic. Even though Dominic and I had a moment, and he's clearly a hero to animals, I can't let myself get close. I'm good at my job too, and I've worked too hard to give it up. I'm going back to LA as soon as the strike's over. That'll be easier without messy entanglements. My heart sinks. Sometimes it's hard to do the right thing.

I park in front of an old white clapboard house with a sign on the glass door that says Robinson Martial Arts Academy.

I open the glass door and head upstairs to the dojo. There's a small waiting area with a row of black plastic chairs and a cubby section for socks and shoes. I'm a little early. I glance over at a raised blue platform with white flexible ropes surrounding it. Drew is there in uniform, along with a few other adults doing stretches. I spot Audrey when she shifts from behind a tall person, and wave to her.

"Hi, Eve! Join us."

"Be there in a sec." I take off my socks and shoes and put them in a cubby.

I walk around to an opening in the ropes and take a step up to the platform. Ooh, the floor's bouncy. Everyone here's in a white karate uniform except me. Guess they'll know who the newbie is.

Drew walks over to me and offers his hand, giving me a firm handshake. "Glad you could make it, Eve. We're just warming up while we wait for everyone to arrive."

"Sure."

"This is the beginner class, so you should be able to keep up. Audrey's here to help guide you if you need it. She recently moved to the more advanced class."

"Aww, Audrey, thank you! You didn't have to do that."

She bounces a little on her feet. "Happy to help."

I go over to her and give her arm a squeeze. "How did things go on Saturday with Dominic, I mean, at the animal tent after I left?" I nearly cringe. I shouldn't care if Audrey has a thing for Dominic or vice versa. I'm just so torn— missing Dominic yet needing to keep my distance for both our sakes.

Drew's head swivels toward us, and I get the sense he's listening.

Audrey twists her arms side to side, warming up. "Great. I'll be volunteering at the shelter on Saturday afternoons. He especially needed someone to handle the cats there. Most people come in wanting to adopt a dog, and the cats don't get enough attention."

Her cheeks flush as Drew walks over to her, looking serious. "Have you been practicing your *katas*? Your test is next week. I can review them with you after class if you want."

She gives him a tight smile. "No need for extra help, *sensei*. I practice on my own just fine. I know the *katas*, and I'm ready."

"Good." He takes his time walking to the front of the space in front of a long mirror. Once there, he faces the mirror and runs through what looks like a choreographed series of punches and kicks.

"That's the first *kata*," she tells me in a low voice. "He's doing it for my benefit. The man is beyond aggravating."

This is really starting to feel like one of those romantic movies where the heroine finds the man aggravating, but it's really just frustrated sexual tension that explodes when they finally connect. Is it that? I rack my brain for a casual way to ask if she's into Drew or Dominic because it's very confusing. It could just be me. Sometimes I make movies out of real-life situations when it's just ordinary life.

She leans toward me, saying in an annoyed voice, "He babies me. He thinks of me like a little sister."

"Guess it's hard when you grow up with someone to see them differently."

She presses her lips in a flat line. "Yup. That's where you have the advantage. I know you're here for him; most of the women are." She gestures toward the waiting area, where three women in their thirties are taking off their shoes and socks. "They never leave the beginner class because they want him to give them one-on-one help for the basic holds."

"Ah. I'm just here to learn."

She slowly lowers into a split position, stretching her legs, only going halfway to the floor. I think I can do that.

I attempt the same, but my legs protest the movement, and then I get stuck. *Ouch, ouch, ouch.* Guess I need to work on my flexibility. I mostly walk and sit at a desk. Crap! I think I'm pulling something in my leg.

I struggle on my own for a few moments before whispering, "Help."

Audrey immediately helps me straighten out of my half-split, which isn't easy because she's petite, maybe five feet one at the most, and I tower above her at five feet ten.

"Thanks," I say, embarrassed.

"I didn't know they do splits in karate," a deep voice says from the waiting area, sounding amused.

I whirl to find Dominic standing next to the platform.

His gaze smolders into mine. A shiver runs down my spine, and goosebumps break out on my arms. My heart thumps an eager beat. I'm way too happy to see him again.

9

I can't take my eyes off Dominic as he approaches. Do I look as happy as I feel? I need to bring it down a notch. I should warm up or something. I can't seem to move.

"I didn't think you'd need a beginners class," Audrey says to him. "You were in the Marines, after all."

I didn't know that.

"I'm a bit rusty," Dominic says. "Thought it'd be good to have a refresher."

I force my gaze from his face and find myself staring at his bicep. It's hard to miss. His T-shirt is tight and barely covers the bulge of his biceps. He's wearing shorts, the muscles in his legs defined. My eye catches on the scar on his knee. We both have scars on our left knees and had the same surgery, but we never shared how we got them. Mostly because I didn't want to talk about mine, and he wasn't keen to relive his memory either. I bet it was when he was in the military. For some reason, it makes me see him differently. He's not just a warm competent guy who loves animals. He was a soldier, brave and strong.

"Maybe you could give me a few pointers," he says to Audrey with a warm smile.

I shift away, uncomfortable witnessing the easy rapport

they share. I've never had that with a guy. Part of me wishes I could with Dominic.

"No problem," she says. "I'm going for my orange belt next week."

"Good for you," he says. "Guess I'm what you call a tan belt."

"A white belt," she says.

"Right. I'll have to get me one of those."

Drew and his assistant roll a few freestanding punching bags onto the mat. Cool. I immediately head over to one and start punching.

Drew stops me with a palm up. "You want to hold your fist like this," he says, demonstrating on his own fist. He waits for me to get it right, and then demonstrates the proper form for a powerful punch.

I take another stab at it with my version of a power punch.

"Better," he says, going to stand by my side. "More like this." Our gazes collide up close, and that familiar concealed pain in his eyes grabs me by the throat. I want to ask what tortures him. Is it PTSD from his time as an Army Ranger? Does he know that Dominic runs a program with therapy dogs to help veterans with PTSD? How is he coping?

"Are you okay?" I blurt.

He steps back. "Never better. Why?"

My hand goes to my heart, an empathetic ache reverberating deep within me. Maybe it's because I've struggled with my own demons. I want to help him. *Don't suffer in silence, Drew. It helps no one.*

He glances at my hand on my heart. "Are *you* okay?"

I attempt a smile. "Maybe we could go out sometime and talk."

"Talk?"

"We could take Jenna's dogs for a walk. Do you like dogs?" *Would you like a therapy dog?*

He stares at me for a quizzical moment. "Yes, I like dogs. Practice your form. Class starts in a few minutes." With that, he walks to the front of the room.

I glance up to find both Audrey and Dominic staring at me. I punch the bag a few times, feeling like a badass. Then I really get into it and start hopping around like a real boxer and use both arms. Fuck cancer. *Bam!* Stupid producers association trying to strong-arm us while they're making the big bucks off our brilliance. One-two combination punch! Men who won't get out of your head! Get! Out! *Bam-bam-bam-bam!*

A loud whistle rings out, and I still. It's Drew, gesturing for me to rejoin the group. It's mostly women here to admire their gorgeous teacher. And then there's Dominic looking so fit you just know he doesn't belong here. My lips press in a flat line. I bet he's trying to make me jealous with Audrey. Totally not going to work.

"Pair up," Drew says. "We're going to work on a few holds and how to break them."

Audrey and Dominic immediately pair up, smiling at each other. I'm *not* jealous.

I pair up with a pretty redhead, one of the trio whom Audrey said only come to class for Drew. I glance at her hand and see she's wearing a wedding band. "How do you like class so far?"

She smiles, her eyes sparkling with amusement. "We're just here for the eye candy. Marcy over there thinks Drew could be a model."

"But you're married."

"Married not dead."

"Ah."

"Ladies, chat on your own time!" Drew barks.

The women all snap to attention. *Drew is really inspiring my kickass heroine for my next screenplay. Dark, commanding, badass.*

I practice a hold with the red-haired lady, who tells me her name is Carla as she chokes me from behind. I'm pretty proud of myself for breaking the hold.

Dominic is super gentle with Audrey when he chokes her and immediately drops his hold when she attempts to break free.

"Do it like you mean it next time," I yell over to him. "You're not doing her any favors going easy on her."

All eyes turn to me.

Dominic looks amused; everyone else looks horrified.

"Maybe you'd like to show everyone the right way," Dominic taunts me.

"Come on up here, Dominic," Drew says. "We'll show the class the right way."

Dominic swaggers to the front of the room, and my heart races double time because they look like two alphas about to show off for Audrey, and one of them could get hurt. They face each other with fierce expressions. The testosterone level shoots through the roof.

The women nearby whisper to each other. Audrey's eyes are wide. I'm not sure whom she's rooting for.

Drew gestures Dominic closer. "Let's show Audrey how to break a hold when your partner's not soft."

Burn.

Dominic stiffens. "Excuse me for not throttling a sweet woman."

"You're supposed to help her learn to defend herself properly," Drew snarls.

Dominic cocks his head to the side. "All right. Let's show her how it's done."

Drew wraps his arm around Dominic's neck from behind.

"Are we starting now?" Dominic asks in a mocking tone.

Drew tightens his hold. Dominic twists out of it and then sweeps Drew's legs out from under him. Drew hits the mat and then pops back up, grabbing Dominic and tossing him to the mat. Dominic pops up like a spring. They face off, circling each other like two alpha lions.

Yeah, Dominic doesn't need to be in beginners class. I suspect the Marines might've taught him a few martial arts skills.

"Are we in a combat situation here, guys?" I yell as I rush to the front of the room.

They break apart, facing me.

Drew scrubs a hand over his face. "Five-minute break, everyone." He strides off the mat and disappears around the corner into what I assume is his office. A door slams shut.

I turn to Dominic, sending him a judgey look for upsetting our teacher.

He lifts his palms. "What? He asked me to demonstrate. Was I not supposed to break the hold?"

"You were showing off, taking him down. Who're you trying to impress?"

Audrey appears by my side. "Are you hurt?" she asks Dominic, all sweet concern. "Drew was Special Forces in the Army, so he might be a little rougher than you're used to."

Dominic looks offended. "I'm a Marine, Audrey. I can handle myself."

She nods. "Maybe you could show me how you did that feet-sweep thing. It wasn't like the takedowns I've learned."

"Sure." He goes with her to where they stood before and starts teaching her.

Okey-doke. I'll just mosey back here to my punching bag. I need to get me one of these. I get into a rhythm, letting all my stress funnel into powerful punches.

A few minutes later, Drew rejoins the class. "Let's get back to work."

The rest of the class goes smoothly. Drew refuses to look at Dominic or Audrey the entire time, his focus entirely on me and the other ladies. I don't mind. He's actually really helpful teaching us how to punch and kick for the most force and, more importantly, *where* to punch and kick in different scenarios.

Class ends, and everyone bows to Drew and thanks him for class with a sharp, "Thank you, *sensei*!" Even Dominic. Not me. I don't bow to anyone.

I walk off the mat and head for my socks and shoes. If I were going to stick around Summerdale, I might sign up for more lessons both for self-defense and research for my screenplay idea.

I overhear Dominic and Audrey talking behind me.

"You should send your book out," Dominic says. "It sounds fascinating. I don't think a soldier story has ever been told with a female lead before. I bet they make it into a movie too."

"Thanks, but it's not ready," she says.

I step out of their way as they get their socks and shoes. They're so engrossed in conversation they don't even notice me.

Drew appears at my side. "Good work today, Eve. I hope you return."

"I would, but I don't know how long I'll be in town."

"We can go week by week," he says distractedly, his eyes on Audrey.

"That might…" I trail off, realizing I don't have his attention anymore.

"I couldn't help but overhear about your book, Aud," Drew says. "What's holding you back?"

Audrey pulls her ponytail forward and twirls the end. She has long brown hair that goes nearly to her waist. "I don't know."

"You know," he says.

"She said she doesn't know," Dominic says, leaping to her defense.

Audrey looks between the two men. "It's just not ready yet."

I head downstairs and step outside, leaving her to her admirers. A moment later, I hear a thundering of footsteps and glance back. Audrey's practically running out the door.

We step out to the sidewalk together.

"Are you okay?" I ask.

She's a little out of breath. "Yeah. Did you like class?"

"It was—"

Drew appears next to us outside. My lord, the man is like a ninja. I didn't even hear the door open.

"Audrey, I have something to say to you, and I want you to listen," he says.

Her hand goes to her throat. "Okay."

"I know your book's good enough because you wrote it. You should send it out."

She drops her hand. "You can't know that. It needs another polish."

"Let me read it. I love military histories, so it's in my wheelhouse. I can even fact-check it for you."

She studies him for a long moment, seeming to consider it.

"It wouldn't be the first time I've read your stuff," he says. "I used to read lots of emails from you, and I liked them."

Her jaw drops. "Drew."

"I did."

"Those emails were so goofy, from an overexcited teen."

He steps closer, his voice turning husky. "I never thought they were goofy. They helped get me through a difficult time."

Her eyes turn soft. "Oh."

"Besides, why did you spend so much time writing your book if you never wanted anyone to read it. Once it's published, anyone can read it."

Her lips curve up, her eyes hopeful. "You really think it'll be published?"

"Absolutely."

"Okay, I'll email it to you." She smiles. "I have to warn you, it's long. Four hundred pages."

He meets her eyes intently. "I'll stay up all night to finish it."

"Wow," she says. "You don't have to do that."

"I have insomnia anyway."

Drew here isn't much of a flirt.

"Right," Audrey says. "Sorry to hear it. Maybe my book will put you to sleep."

He shakes his head. "Doubt it."

The door opens, and Dominic appears, joining us. "Now that was some class."

Drew narrows his eyes at him suspiciously. "You've had training. Why're you at a beginners class?"

Dominic turns to Audrey. "She said I should come."

Audrey beams.

Drew mumbles something under his breath and heads back inside.

"I'd better go," I say, turning toward the parking lot.

"Bye, Eve," Audrey says. "I'll see you tomorrow at Jenna's house. We're taking ladies' night to her place since she and Paige just had babies. You and I can enjoy a nice pinot grigio while the nursing ladies sip their sparkling water."

"Sounds good." I do enjoy a glass of wine now and then with friends.

I get into my car. Dominic stares at me through the windshield. I give him a small wave, power the car on, and back out of the lot. My heart aches again, leaving him behind, but I know it's for the best.

I hit the accelerator when I get to Route 15, the only road with a forty-five-mile-per-hour speed limit in town. A large red building catches my eye, and I glance over at it. Oh, it's the animal shelter behind the animal hospital. My car hits a jarring bump as I hit a pothole I didn't see. And then it's hard to steer, the car shaking violently. Shit. I think I have a flat tire. I slow down and pull over to the side of the road.

I put my hazards on and step out to inspect the passenger-side tire. It's dark out here. Fortunately, there's a streetlight not far from my car. There aren't too many on this road or anywhere in town. The road is surrounded by woods on either side with the occasional house. I shiver as every horror movie flashes through my head. The woods. A dark night. A lone woman stranded on the side of the road.

I dig my phone out of my purse and shine light on the tire. Yup, it's flat all right.

A red Dodge Challenger pulls up behind me. A classic muscle car. Great. Just what I need, some beefy guy coming to "rescue" a woman in distress. I may not be able to change my own tire, but I can damn well call triple A. And I know karate. Sort of.

Dominic steps out. My heart beats double time. *He showed up when I needed him.*

Just a coincidence, right? It's not like I texted him for help.

When he reaches me, he's got a smug look on his gorgeous face. "First you stalk me across an entire country, then you call me for an animal emergency, you show up in my free karate class, and now you have a road emergency in front of my place. If I didn't know better, I'd say you were into me, Eve Larsen."

I close the distance between us, breathing in the scent of clean male skin with a hint of his cologne, my heart hammering. I blurt out my last worry. "What about Audrey? You two seem close."

"Audrey's into Drew."

A warm glow builds deep within me. "Not that it's my business."

He pushes a lock of hair behind my ear, a tender gesture that undoes me, making my knees weak. "So make it your business."

10

Dominic

Eve licks her lips, her eyes dropping to my mouth before she jerks her gaze back to my eyes. I know that look, and I like it. "I need to call triple A."

"You don't need them. You've got me." I walk over to her car. "Pop the trunk for me."

She hesitates for a moment and then decides to take me up on my gallant gesture. I can do basic car maintenance. Dad taught me and my brothers how to fix stuff. He was in sales, but so handy around the house he remodeled our kitchen and added a sunroom by himself.

I pull the spare tire, jack, and lug wrench from the trunk and head over to the flat, getting down to business.

"My dad showed me how to do this once," she says. "I just have trouble getting the lug nuts off the tire."

"Yeah, they can be tough." I lever the first one loose. "Think you'll continue in karate while you're here?"

"Why were you there?"

"Same reason as you were. I was invited."

Eve's lips press into a flat line. "I don't know how long I'll be in town." She starts pacing on the side of the road.

Truth is, I went to class knowing Eve would be there with

Drew. I've stewed over that long enough. Eve didn't flirt with him at all.

After I finish with the tire, I stand and stretch my back. "All done. You should take it to Murray's for a new tire."

"It's a rental. I'll have to call the rental car company first. Maybe they'll just give me a different car."

I put everything back in the trunk, including the damaged tire, and shut it.

"Thank you for your help," she says.

"You're welcome." I step closer. I want to touch her, stroke her cheek, trace her jaw. I only resist because my hands are dirty from the tire. "You want to stop by my place for a drink? I live in the apartment over the animal hospital."

She looks across the street at my place. "Short commute."

"Sure is."

"Aren't the animals noisy downstairs?"

"Most of the animals are at the shelter farther back. It's only an occasional overnight surgical patient downstairs. If they're making noise, I want to hear it so I can check on them. Generally, they sleep. Henry's back at home now, in case you're wondering."

She stares at my place again. "That's great."

"Eve, come to my place. I have your favorite on tap. Water."

She waves airily. "I'm just going for a friendly drink. Nothing's going to happen."

Hope surges through me. "Okay."

"I mean it."

"I know."

I go back to my car and wait for her to get into hers. Not much traffic, so I'm able to follow her out. A few minutes later, Eve parks in the small graveled lot to the side of the house, and I pull in next to her. There's a circular driveway for clients with additional parking on the other side.

I guide her to the back entrance that leads to the stairs to my place. It's basic—living room, kitchen, bedroom, and bathroom. One day I'd like to buy a house separate from work, but at the moment most of my money is tied up in the practice I took over.

I unlock the door to my apartment and flip on the light switch. "Here we are."

She steps inside and looks around the living room. It's just a beige sofa, coffee table, and end tables with reading lamps. I mostly read about the latest techniques in veterinary medicine. My dog, PJ, blinks owlishly at us from his bed next to the sofa, where he's curled up.

"PJ!" she exclaims. "You adopted him."

"Sure did. He goes to work with me and sleeps and then comes home with me and sleeps."

"Aww! That's great." She scoops him up and cuddles him close, rubbing her cheek against the top of his little head. He tolerates it. Barely.

"Let me take him out to do his business," I say. "Make yourself comfortable."

She sets him down. "Go see Dominic."

PJ heads straight to his bed, turning in a circle as he always does before settling down.

"No," Eve says. "Outside, PJ. You've got business to take care of."

I go over and pick him up. Boston terriers can be stubborn. He mostly only does what he feels like.

"He's not a great listener, is he?" she asks.

"I suspect he only understands Spanish."

"Really?"

I grin.

She shakes her head, smiling, and looks around before settling on the sofa.

I take PJ out, let him sniff out the perfect patch of grass near a tree before finally peeing, and bring him back inside. He goes right back to bed. Eve leans over the side of the sofa to talk to him and pet him.

I head for the kitchen, wash my hands, and pour a glass of water. When I return with the water, she says, "Where's the TV?"

I hand her the glass of water. "I don't have one."

"You don't have one?" she practically shouts.

PJ's ears lift, but he's too tired to lift his head.

"Is that a problem?" I ask, sitting next to her.

"You know I'm a TV writer."

"You mentioned it."

She stares at me. "You've never seen *Irreverent*."

It's not a question. "If it makes you feel better, I could get a TV. I usually stream something on the laptop if I feel like vegging out."

"Vegging out? There's a lot of great, fascinating content out there right now. Real sharp writing, twisty plots, fantastic characters."

Somehow I've insulted her and her entire profession. "I'm sure *Irreverent* is great. We could watch it if you want."

"I wrote episode two this season."

"If it's important to you, I'll watch it."

She scowls. "Clearly it's not important to you."

Was I supposed to get a TV in case she came over one day?

"Eve, are we having our first fight? That would imply more than a one-night thing."

She throws her hands up. "This was a mistake. You should be with someone who's sticking around." She sets her glass on the coffee table before walking to the door. "I don't even know why I'm here."

I race after her. Just as she reaches for the knob, I put my palms against the door over her shoulders, keeping it closed.

She whirls, facing me, her eyes flashing. "Dominic!"

"*I* know why you're here."

Her eyes widen, her breath hitching. "I'm not what you're looking for."

I cradle her jaw, stroking her soft cheek. "I wasn't looking at all. Tell me you don't want this, and I'll leave you alone." I kiss her gently, and then again and again.

She lets out a soft sigh and throws her arms around my neck, kissing me back hungrily. I wrap my arms around her, taking over the kiss, tasting her sweet mouth. Lust fires through me. I've never wanted anyone the way I want her.

She breaks the kiss. "What're we doing?"

"I don't know." I kiss her lips, her cheek, her jaw. Her fingers slide through my hair, her head tilting to the side, giving me better access as I kiss a trail to her throat. I bite softly down her neck. She moans, her hands roaming over my back. I return to her mouth, feasting on the luscious feel and taste of her. I pull her closer, and she hitches her leg up, pressing against me. Need claws at me.

I pull back to look at her.

She's breathing heavily, her eyes dilated. "Don't stop."

I scoop her up, carrying her into the bedroom.

She giggles. "I've never been carried to bed before. This is just like in the movies."

"It's expedient," I say, lowering her to the mattress.

She opens her arms to me. My breath catches, my heart doing a quick tumble. I join her, our bodies fitting together perfectly as I kiss and taste every inch of exposed skin, taking my time.

Her kiss becomes more demanding as she pulls at my clothes. I remove them quickly and make short work of hers. And then we're kissing, rolling over the bed, her on top, and then me. Nothing matters but skin on skin. I can't get enough of her. Soft skin, long-limbed toned muscle, her silky hair, her scent like vanilla, so delicious.

And when we finally join, it's like sliding home. I cradle her face, kissing her and sucking on her lower lip. She bucks her hips under me, and then it's nothing but a wild ride as every movement, every soft moan urges me on. The moment I feel her shudder with release, I lose all control, pounding into her, my own release exploding through me.

I collapse on top of her, breathing heavily.

"Wow," she says.

I lift my head. "Wow."

"I can't spend the night. Jenna's expecting me to help in the morning."

I shift to my side, stroking idly across her shoulder. "Text her that you'll be back by seven in the morning. That's when I get up for work. It's still early."

She rolls to her side, facing me. "I haven't had a relationship in a long time. I'm divorced after several awful relationships. And the long distance sorta puts an expiration date on whatever this is."

"My divorce was enough to put me off relationships too. Let's just spend time together while you're here and not worry about the future."

She sighs and runs her palm over my bicep.

"We could watch *Irreverent*," I add.

She smiles, her eyes lighting up. My heart thumps harder. "Yeah?"

I nuzzle into her neck and whisper huskily in her ear, "Among other things."

~

Eve

A warm male hand rests against my bare stomach as Dominic spoons me from behind. I'm groggy but awake as light filters through the blinds. I probably slept three hours total last night, and it wasn't just for mind-blowing, toe-curling sex. We watched *Irreverent*, and Dominic loved my episode. We talked a lot, too, comparing East Coast to West Coast living; he told me about his family and growing up in Michigan; I even shared about my complicated relationship with Mom and how we're trying to connect again before it's too late. Sometimes you think you have all the time in the world with someone, but life is fragile. You just never know.

I stroke his forearm, not wanting to leave this warm bed. It's tough for me to open up to another person, yet I let myself be vulnerable with him. I feel like we really got to know each other last night. It's a good feeling. The best part is that I don't have to worry about messing up the relationship. It'll end naturally, not because of something I screwed up. I know

I'll be sad when the time comes, but I'm trying to just enjoy the moment, like he said, and not think about the future.

I like him, *really* like him.

His hand runs down my side and over my hip. "Morning," he whispers in my ear.

I look over my shoulder at him. "Morning. I'm so tired."

He lifts my leg up and over his legs, opening me to him. "So let's stay in bed a little longer."

"You're insatiable."

His fingers delve between my legs, circling lightly over the magic spot, as his erection presses against me from behind, teasing but not entering me. I moan softly. He pays close attention and knows what I like. I close my eyes, letting the rush of sensation take over.

His voice is a deep rumble in my ear. "I love feeling you let go, Eve. It's a beautiful thing."

I press back against him. "Take me."

"Not yet. I want to play with you some more." His hand shifts to caress my breast, circling the tip and then pinching it gently.

"Dominic, I need you," I practically beg.

He jerks away suddenly. Bewildered, I roll to my back to look at him.

"Hi, Daddy," a small little-girl voice says.

11

I yelp and dive under the covers. *Daddy?* Dominic is a dad? With all the sharing we did last night about ourselves and our families, he never once mentioned he had a daughter. I can't believe he didn't mention it. Did he think it wasn't important? Jesus. What kind of a dad is he?

Dominic sits up, adjusting the covers around him. His voice is gentle. "Hi, Nora. How did you get in here?"

A throaty feminine voice answers, "I made a copy of the key from when you let us stay here over the Fourth of July."

Dominic's quiet for a stunned moment. I can already tell this woman is a piece of work.

"I'll need that back, Lexi," he says sharply. "Give us a minute."

Lexi is his ex-wife. He mentioned her last night. Only that she left him for her sister's ex-husband, no mention of a kid. My gut twists. It was a lie by omission, but still a lie. The one time I trust a man, I'm instantly shown why I can't.

The blanket pulls half off me, and I pop my head out to grab it. A little girl with dark hair that falls to her shoulders with sky-blue eyes is attempting to get into the bed by climbing the blanket. I'm guessing she's two or three.

Dominic sits up. "Nora, let go of the blanket. I need to get out of bed and get dressed."

She lets go and stares at his bare chest. "Where's your pajamas, Daddy?"

I grit my teeth and glare at Lexi. She gives me a sly smile. She's pretty in that way that says she spends a lot of time at the salon and the dermatologist. Flawless skin, straight glossy black hair, perfect makeup. I hate her already. Seriously, who sends a toddler into someone's bedroom? She must've heard us in here.

"Come on, honey," she says, taking Nora by the hand. "We'll tell Daddy our big news after he's had his coffee. Grownups are always grumpy before they have their coffee."

The door shuts behind them. I stare at Dominic mutely, waiting for an explanation.

He closes his eyes for a moment. "I know."

"How could you not mention you have a daughter?"

"I'm new at this. I didn't know when to bring it up."

"Maybe sometime during our marathon three-hour talk?" I roll out of bed and grab my clothes. "God, the one time I trust a guy enough to actually open up, and you weren't opening up at all." I yank my clothes on quickly.

"I only found out about her on Father's Day when Lexi brought Nora to meet me after her stepdad died."

I gather my socks and shoes and purse. "So you've known for four whole months that you have a daughter, and it's still not something you talk about?"

"I don't know what I'm doing, okay?" he barks.

"Obviously! How could you not know about her before then?"

"Because when Lexi walked out, she told me she was pregnant by the guy she left me for. I was too shocked to question it and didn't stay in touch with her."

"So how do you know Nora's really yours?"

"I got a paternity test this time."

I jam my hands in my hair. "This is so fucked up. I can't even believe I thought for once—you know what, forget it. Don't call me."

I race out the door, so eager to escape I don't even reply when Lexi says mockingly, "Nice to meet you too."

Fucking men with their secrets. Their lies and betrayals. This, this right here, is why I avoided relationships for so long. Is it so much to ask for an honest man who shows up for you?

My gut churns, nausea rising in my throat. I never want to see him again.

∼

Dominic

I throw some clothes on, brush my teeth, and splash cold water on my face. I'm pissed that Lexi showed up here unannounced and sent little Nora in, knowing I wasn't alone in bed. She must've seen Eve's car parked outside, not to mention we weren't exactly quiet. Poor Eve. I get that she was surprised by the news, and I don't blame her for fleeing the scene. I just hope she won't shut me out forever. I'm still getting used to the fact that I actually have a kid. I don't know when or how to mention it to people because that involves a story I'm not keen to share.

I open the door to the bedroom, and PJ darts inside, heading for the bed I keep here for him. Guess he wants to avoid the scene as much as I do.

I find Nora sitting on the sofa, watching something on Lexi's phone, her gaze glued to it without even blinking. Nora's too young to watch TV, only two, but I don't get much say in the matter. Ever since I found out about her, I've been trying to get joint custody. The most I've gotten is supervised Sunday visits every other week at Lexi's apartment in the city. New York City being the city around here.

"I got the coffeemaker started for you," Lexi says cheerfully. "You really need to get better quality coffee." Her voice, which I used to find sexy, is like claws scraping against my insides. Horrific.

I clench my jaw and keep my voice civil for Nora's sake.

"You have to let me know when you're stopping by for a visit." I hold out my palm. "Give me the key. You shouldn't have copied it without my permission."

She huffs and goes to her purse at the small breakfast bar that separates the kitchen from the living room and pulls the key off her keychain. "Here. I don't see what the big deal is."

I stuff the key in my pocket. "The big deal is this is my private space, and you can't invade it whenever you want!" My voice gets loud at the end.

Nora looks over at us. "Hungry."

Lexi grabs a snack container of Cheerios from her purse and hands it to her.

I help myself to a mug of coffee and try to order my thoughts. I want Lexi gone as quickly as possible. At the same time, I need to stay on good terms with her if I want to keep seeing Nora.

I take a sip of black coffee and lean back against the counter.

Lexi brings a wooden bar stool from the other side of the breakfast bar into the small kitchen and perches on top. "Good news," she chirps.

"What?"

"You're going to be seeing a lot more of Nora."

My heart thunders. Is Lexi leaving Nora here? I glance over at Nora stuffing Cheerios into her mouth one-handed while she holds the phone with her other hand. Cheerios bounce onto her lap and the sofa. I'm not sure I'm ready to be a full-time dad.

"Why is that?" I ask carefully.

She sighs, looking to the ceiling. "I couldn't get her into any of the good preschools in the city." She lowers her voice. "She failed every interview because she won't warm up to the interviewer. She just sits there, refusing to play or speak. It's like she purposely tried to fail."

"She's two. She's not trying to manipulate any situation. They must know how to draw out shy kids. Did you tell them how she loves animals? Maybe let her show them her favorite board book with the animals. She's so smart, she can name all of them, even distinguishing between the gray and white rhinoceroses."

"You can't bring in props. It has to look natural. Anyway, I tried some backchannels to get her in but no go. Without entry into one of the best preschools, she can't get into the best private school for elementary, and it just snowballs from there. All doors are closed to us."

"So you're saying because she's a shy two-year-old, she's doomed for life? What about public school?"

"That's where all the rejected kids go."

I reach for patience. "Maybe she'd like them and vice versa."

"Doesn't matter." She sighs. "Besides, we're shut out. My friends have their new preschool mom friends and their own playgroups. So we adjust and adapt. We're moving."

"Where?"

"Here!"

Worry tempers my joy at having my daughter near. "As in, my place?"

She glances around. "God, no. This place is way too small. I sold my apartment and bought a house by the lake. Hello, neighbor! Now you'll get to see us all the time."

I let out a breath of relief. "That's great. I'd love to see her more. Maybe she could stay with me here on the weekend. We could trade off weekends."

"She's too young for sleepovers. Since Sam died, she's become very attached to me." Nora's stepdad, Sam, believed Nora was his, which was why he married Lexi so quickly. From what I can tell, he was good to Nora.

We both look over at Nora glued to her screen. She doesn't seem so attached to Lexi. I'd believe it if I saw Lexi frequently holding her, or even Nora wanting her to, hanging onto her leg or asking to be picked up.

"Did you find a school for her here?" I ask. "It's October; they've already started."

She smiles. "I did. The Episcopalian preschool had an

opening, and the best part is the public schools here are rated the best in the state. And I'm going back to work. My old boss says I can work part-time from home." Lexi works in pharmaceutical sales.

"Okay, this is good news. I don't appreciate the way you barged in here to share it, but I'm glad to hear it."

She hops off the bar stool and helps herself to a cup of coffee, leaning against the counter next to me. "Who was the blonde? Anyone serious?"

I shake my head, unwilling to share anything about Eve. I don't trust Lexi farther than I could throw her. "She's just visiting her sister in town."

She smiles up at me. "Then maybe this is a chance for a fresh start for us as a family."

I lift my mug to hide a grimace. After a sip of coffee, I say, "I'm looking forward to more time with Nora, but you and I are done for good."

"Mmm-hmm. Okay, I get it. You just climbed out of bed with a leggy blonde. Let's keep an open mind."

I stare at her. "Lexi, you broke my trust when you kept my daughter from me. I missed out on her babyhood completely because you lied and said she wasn't mine. There's no going back to what we had. You destroyed that."

"It might be the best thing for Nora."

"We can coparent, but you and I will never get back together."

Lexi barrels on as if I haven't spoken. "She needs that kind of stability. Do you know ever since Sam died, she's tried to crawl into bed with me every night?"

"You don't let her?"

"I give her a pillow and blanket to sleep on the floor next to me. I only share my bed with my lover."

I suck in air. "She's a little girl hurting from the loss of the only dad she's ever known."

"That's what I'm saying. If we become a family, it would be good for her." She takes a sip of coffee, makes a face, and dumps it in the sink. "I'll bring you some good coffee next time I stop by. Nora, we're going now."

Nora looks up, her gaze going from her mom to me. "Daddy."

I walk over and sit on the sofa next to her. I've been cautious about touching her, letting her come to me instead of just swooping her into my arms like I want to. Kids, I figure, are like animals, needing time to warm up to you. You have to earn their trust.

She looks up at me with wide innocent eyes the color of the sky like mine. "Will you visit my new house?" She speaks really well for her age. She'll be three in a couple of months.

"Not today. I have to work, but I'd love to visit this weekend."

She climbs into my lap and stares at me. "Is a doggy sick again?"

"I'm not sure, but I have to be there to check. Sometimes I get cats or lizards or birds too. Every day is a surprise."

She pats my cheek. "Good vetrium." Veterinarian is a mouthful for her.

"They call me Dr. Russo."

She scrunches up her face. "Dogs can't talk."

I stifle a laugh. "Not the dogs. Their owners call me that."

"Do you give the doggies shots? I hate shots."

"Sometimes I do. It's to keep them healthy just like you."

She squirms off my lap, spilling the Cheerios all over the floor.

"Let's pick these up, Nora," I say.

She bends to the rug to pick them up, popping one in her mouth.

"Don't eat them," I say, holding out the snack container. "Put them in here, and then I'll put them in the trash."

Lexi rushes over and grab's Nora's hand. "No! Those are dirty. Let's go." She scoops her up and heads out the door.

"Bye, Daddy!"

I lean back against the sofa, exhausted. "Bye, Nora."

Eve

I'm putting Dominic behind me. I've now blocked his number, so no more calls or texts. Fortunately, I've been completely involved with Jenna and the baby since that disastrous morning four days ago. I told Jenna all about the surprise morning wakeup from his little girl that he failed to mention. She thinks I should give him a chance to explain, as he asked to do in his texts before I blocked him. After I shared with him about my past, which is not easy for me to do, I expected to learn at least the basics about him. What kind of dad doesn't acknowledge he has a kid?

It's a beautiful Sunday just before noon, and Jenna and I are taking Theo on a stroller walk around Lake Summerdale. Eli's taking a well-deserved break after working a day shift on Saturday and getting up in the night with Theo. I've offered to take some nighttime feedings, but they have the baby's crib in their room so they can get to him quickly and handle it without me. Unfortunately, I still wake when I hear him cry. It's like a very alarming two a.m. alarm clock.

I breathe in the crisp air with just a hint of the winter to come. I don't miss winter, but I do miss the brilliant reds, oranges, and yellows of fall foliage. The lake is the hub of town with streets leading away from it like spokes on a wheel. We're on a paved walking path around the lake.

"The leaves are just starting to turn," Jenna says. "It's Theo's first fall. See the red peeking out over there?" She leans down to check on him in his stroller. He's asleep.

"Looks like if you just keep moving, he'll sleep," I say.

"I'll lose this baby weight in no time," she quips.

"Please. You never had baby weight. It was all baby."

"I've got some. Trust me." She looks suddenly alert. "Dominic," she whispers.

I look up to find Dominic, Lexi, and Nora walking toward us. Nora is between them, holding each of their hands. My gut does a slow churn. They look like a family. I want to turn and walk in the other direction, but there's no getting around this confrontation.

"Hi, Dominic," Jenna says, smiling at him. "Meet baby Theo. He's sleeping."

He takes a peek at the baby. Nora follows him, grabbing the baby's foot through the blanket. Dominic takes her hand out of the stroller. "Congratulations."

"Thanks," she says, looking curiously at Nora.

"This is my daughter, Nora."

Nora clutches his leg, suddenly shy.

Lexi joins us. "I'm Lexi, Nora's mom."

Dominic introduces me and Jenna. Then he says, "Eve, I've been wanting to talk to you."

I work on a neutral expression, hiding how much it pains me to see him like this. "No need. I see you're busy with your family."

"Nice to formally be introduced," Lexi says to me, sounding amused.

I give her a deadeye stare. Nothing funny about barging in on your ex in bed with someone else. A moment of awkward silence is broken by Nora exclaiming, "Ducks!" and racing toward the lake.

Dominic bolts after her. Lexi makes a nonchalant shrug and follows them.

Jenna and I keep walking at a brisk pace. As soon as we're out of earshot, she says, "I see what you mean about Lexi. She sounded like she was mocking you for getting caught naked in bed when she's the one who snuck into the place."

"And sent her toddler in first."

"Nasty woman. Nora resembles Dominic around the eyes. It *is* strange that he never mentioned Nora. I work with him all the time at the shelter and for fundraising activities, and he never said a word. She looks to be two or three. It must've been a shock for him to only meet her a few months ago. Maybe he's still getting used to the idea."

I exhale sharply. "Looks like they're trying to work things out for Nora's sake."

She's quiet for a few moments. "Maybe. But they did get divorced for a reason."

"So did Mom and Dad, and now they're back together."

"Lexi betrayed him, though. I'm not sure it's forgivable, you know? Keeping his kid from him for so long. It sounds like the only reason she told him was because her husband died."

"She probably needed child support." I shake my head. "It's too messy. I don't want to get in the middle of all that. He's got stuff to work out; his daughter needs him; his ex needs him. I don't. I was fine before I met him, and I'll be fine after."

She puts her arm around my shoulders and gives me a sideways hug. "I'm sorry it turned out like this."

My lower lip trembles, and I clamp down on it with my teeth. "Yeah."

"If it helps, he looked like he really wanted to talk to you. Maybe clear some stuff up."

"It doesn't."

12

Three days later, I'm still thinking about Dominic. Part of me wants to talk to him, clear the air, or whatever. Things ended on a really bad note. But then I tell myself there's no point in rehashing the facts. He kept a huge thing from me; therefore, he's not to be trusted. Most men aren't. Besides Dad, I've never had one man show up for me when I needed him. You just can't depend on a man. I knew that, yet like a fool, I trusted again. I'm back at karate class, mostly to punch the shit out of a punching bag.

Drew greets me warmly as soon as I step inside. "Hey, you're back. Can I get you on a weekly schedule?"

"Sure, why not. I'll probably be here at least until the end of October." That's how shitty the strike negotiations are going. Everything in my life is shitty at the moment. Hence, the punching bag.

"Great. Be right back."

I put my socks and shoes in a cubby. A few people on the platform stretch and practice their punches and kicks. Everyone here is a white belt. Audrey's not here. She was promoted to a more advanced class.

I head toward the opening in the ropes to climb onto the platform when Drew intercepts me, holding a neatly folded karate uniform with a white belt on top.

He hands it to me, his eyes intent on mine, all business. "This is your *gi*. Come with me, I'll show you the ladies' changing area, and then we can meet in my office for a few minutes."

"Before I do that, how much is each class?"

"There's a set fee, but if you have financial need, we can work something out. Let's talk in my office."

I follow him to the ladies' changing area, where there's a group of women from last week changing. The married women's club, here for the eye candy. Couldn't they get the same thrill admiring some TV star or a model on the internet? Just saying, it's a lot of time and money to commit to weekly Drew gazing.

I glance sideways at one of the ladies to see if she's wearing anything underneath her *gi*. Okay, she left a T-shirt on underneath. I strip out of my jogging pants and put the white uniform pants on. They're kind of stiff. Next I put on the top over my T-shirt and wrap the belt around me, tying it in a double knot. I glance in a nearby full-length mirror, surprised at how professional I look. I could be lethal with these hands. *Hi-ya!*

"Nice to see you again, Eve," a red-haired woman says to me.

I turn to see her smiling at me. Her two friends give me small waves. "You too. I'm sorry I forgot your names."

They rattle off their names, and I point at them each in turn, trying to cement the names in my mind. "Marcy, Carla, Jen, right?"

"Almost," the short brunette says. "Joan."

"Joan. We should wear name tags in beginner class."

"You'll get it soon," Joan says kindly.

They leave, and I stand there for a moment marveling over how friendly everyone in Summerdale has been to me. It's not like that in LA. I wander over toward Drew's office next door.

He's sitting behind an old wood desk and indicates I should take the plastic chair across from him. He slides a two-page contract across the desk. It's mostly about what Robinson Martial Arts Academy stands for: honor, respect, empowerment, *blah-blah-blah*. I skim through a bunch of legal liability stuff and finally get to the weekly and monthly fees. There's also a discount for a year-long contract. This is actually doable for me on a weekly basis. I'm used to LA prices.

"I'm good with weekly," I say, grabbing a pen from a paper cup on his desk full of pens and signing the contract.

He stands and executes a small bow. "Welcome to Robinson Martial Arts Academy."

I stand and bow too since it's a mutual bowing situation. "Thank you."

"You should call me *sensei*. It means teacher."

He moves from behind the desk and gestures for me to follow him out. "Is your boyfriend joining you today?"

I whirl to face him. "He's not my boyfriend."

His brows scrunch together. "Oh."

I wonder if he's now contemplating if Dominic was here for Audrey, and if I should say that wasn't the case, but then I decide it's best if I just stay out of the whole Drew-Audrey thing.

I step onto the mat. The ladies from the locker room follow a moment later.

Drew jogs to the front of the space and rubs his hands together. "Let's get started, class."

"Yes, *sensei*!" we all say together.

After class, I'm feeling good, pumped from my workout. I really gave the punching bag a sound thrashing with my powerful punches and kicks.

Drew appears by my side as I walk back toward the ladies' changing area. "Good work today, Eve. Your form was much better on your punches."

"Thank you, *sensei*."

"You can call me Drew when we're off the mat."

I glance at him. He's not smiling, but his eyes seem less guarded. Is this the beginning of a friendship? Maybe I could ask him more about his background for my screenplay research.

"How're Jenna and the baby doing?" he asks.

"Great. Jenna's doing so well with him. Theo's amazing."

"Course he is. He's a Robinson." Theo's his nephew.

I smile. "You should stop by to visit him this weekend. We do takeout on Saturday nights with my parents. The more the merrier."

"Maybe I will."

I smile as I reach the ladies' changing area. He backs up a step and then whirls in a defensive posture to face the three women I met earlier. Whoa. Some killer reflexes there.

"Hi, *sensei*," Marcy says with a giggle. "Great class today."

The other women rush to agree.

"Glad to hear it." He escapes into his office.

I change quickly, my thoughts returning to Dominic again. I wish I could get him out of my head. And my heart. Damn him. I wouldn't be so twisted up over him if he hadn't gotten into my heart.

I say bye to the ladies and head to the waiting room for my socks and shoes.

Just as I'm finishing lacing my sneakers, the door opens. Before I even look up, part of me knows. I meet Dominic's eyes, my heart racing, my nerves instantly on edge, raw and vulnerable.

He showed up.

Doesn't matter. He lied and can't be trusted.

"I hoped to find you here," he says. "Can we talk? I'd like to explain."

"Dominic, you don't have to explain anything to me." *Because it's over.*

I head for the door. He holds it for me, letting me go downstairs ahead of him. He follows behind and catches up with me on the sidewalk.

"One drink," he says, tucking a lock of hair behind my ear.

He's close enough his delicious scent washes over me, making me weak in the knees. Clean soap, ocean, and something distinctly sexy Dominic.

I let out a shaky sigh. This is the only man who's managed to get past my defenses in ages. And if it was just sex, I'd be done by now. "Okay, one drink. At The Horseman Inn. I've seen what one drink at your place will lead to."

He strokes my hair back from my face, his lips grazing my temple. "Thank you."

~

Dominic and I meet in the parking lot of The Horseman Inn. It's a short drive. He holds the door of the restaurant open for me, and I walk through on stiff legs. I don't know why I'm opening myself up for more hurt. We made no promises to each other. Whatever he has to say shouldn't matter in the least.

I slow my step, and his hand presses on my lower back, guiding me forward.

A few moments later, we're seated in a corner table in the back dining room. It's quiet in here on a Wednesday night, and we're the only people in the back room. There's a few guys watching the game on the TV above the bar. As far as a neutral setting, you couldn't get any better.

A waitress in her sixties with dyed blond hair stops by our table. "Hi, Dr. Russo."

"Hi, Ellen, how's Tiger?" He probably knows everyone in town by their pets.

"He's doing much better now, thanks. Bounced right back."

"Glad to hear it," Dominic says.

Ellen turns to me. "You must be Jenna's sister, Eve. You look just like her."

I smile. "That's right. Nice to meet you."

"Kitchen closes in half an hour if you want something to eat. Otherwise, the bar's open until ten."

"Just sparkling water for me," I say.

"I'll have the same," Dominic says.

She tilts her head. "You got it."

Dominic switches seats to sit next to me. "Listen, I'm sorry you had to find out about Nora that way. Lexi had no right to barge in like that."

My gut churns. "It's not like we made any promises to each other."

"Still, it wasn't right."

I stare at the table, a lump of emotion caught in my throat. I don't know how or when, but somehow Dominic got to me. I hate feeling vulnerable like this.

He tilts my chin up, forcing me to look at him. "I'm still getting used to the idea that I have a kid, and I wasn't sure when to bring it up. I didn't know if we had a future together, or even if it would drive you away."

"I wouldn't have held it against you if you'd been honest."

"I'm rusty at this relationship stuff and new at the dad thing. That's my only excuse."

I'm still not sure I can trust him. "This was a pretty big thing to keep secret. What else haven't you told me?"

"I don't know, Eve. What else haven't you told me?"

"I told you about my parents," I choke out. Though I haven't shared the shame over my accident and the addiction that followed. Not to mention the details of the horrible string of relationships during that time and my divorce. I got myself into some bad situations. It was hard enough to open up about one thing, and then I was slammed with this giant surprise.

He rubs my back in a soothing gesture. "I'm sure there's more we could get to know about each other given time. As long as you're here, I'd like that. I just didn't know what to say about Nora or when. Again, I'm sorry about the way you found out."

I stare at the table, my throat tight. "You looked like a family when I saw you by the lake on Sunday. I don't want to get in the way of that. It's not fair to Nora." I swallow hard and force myself to meet his eyes. "I'm not sure this was a good idea."

"You said one drink. We didn't have our drink yet."

I glance over to see Ellen approaching with our glasses of sparkling water. I force a pleasant expression, even though my insides are churning. She sets water in front of me. "Thank you."

"You're welcome," she says. "And for you." She sets Dominic's water down. "Sure you don't want anything to eat?"

"We're good," Dominic says.

She nods and walks away. I'm actually really thirsty after karate class, so I go ahead and drink while he starts to talk. I steel myself to keep a neutral expression. I don't want to let on just how difficult talking about that night is because then he'll know I care too much.

"Eve, I never like to share much about my divorce because, frankly, it's humiliating. Bad enough she cheated on me, but then to also be pregnant with his baby. It makes me look like a fool."

"Only she lied."

"You can imagine how shocked I was at the time and hurt. I never questioned it and, in hindsight, I should have." He runs a shaky hand through his hair. "That should've been me with Nora from the beginning not Sam."

I want to comfort him, wrap my arms around him and take the pain away, but I'm frozen in place. "You're right."

"Sam died last May doing what he loved—racing. I didn't know him well. I'd only met him once before. He was divorced from Lexi's sister by the time I got together with Lexi."

Curiosity gets the better of me. "How did you and Lexi meet?"

"Sort of random at a party. She was a friend of a friend. I'd just started veterinary school. We married after only a few months of dating and divorced just shy of our two-year anniversary."

"I only made it through one year of marriage. He was in love with another woman, so there was no point."

"That must have been hard."

"Not as bad as what you went through."

He exhales sharply and looks to the ceiling. "True. In any case, I didn't know about Nora until the month after Sam died. Lexi surprised me on Father's Day with the news and introduced us. The whole time I'm staring in awe at my daughter, Lexi is going on about child support since she was looking at a major change in lifestyle with the death of her husband. He had life insurance, but not enough for Lexi to continue spending as she wanted."

"Sorry, I'm not trying to be judgmental, but what did you ever see in Lexi? She sounds like a money-grubber."

He lets out a mirthless laugh. "She grew up poor and clawed her way out. I get that. But before we married, she was just…fun, up for anything. Everything was light and easy, and she looked at me like I was her world." He gives me a wry look. "I thought that meant we'd go the distance. She showed her true colors after we married, spending money we didn't have, always harping on me to make connections in a wealthy area for my job after graduation. After only six months, things had frayed between us. She just never seemed happy. I tried to make it work, but I was also balancing a ton of schoolwork. I can't say it was all her fault the marriage fell apart. She was lonely."

"That's no excuse for what she did."

He presses his lips together grimly. "Agreed. In any case, Lexi introduced me to Nora as Daddy. I thought it would be confusing for her, but Nora just went with it. She's two and a half, three this December. I have to wonder if Sam hadn't died, if I ever would've known I had a daughter." His voice chokes.

I squeeze his hand. "It's such a betrayal. Worse than just cheating because a child is involved."

He takes a sip of water and heaves a sigh. "I suspected she was mine when I saw her eyes, but I still got proof with a paternity test. She's got Lexi's face. It made me wonder if it was a boy if he would've looked more like me. Not that I'm not thrilled with a daughter." A soft look comes over his eyes. "She's amazing."

He loves her, and I'm glad for it. At the same time, I know I don't belong in this picture.

"It sounds like a complicated situation," I say gently. "The last thing I want is to get caught up in the middle."

"You won't be. That life will be separate from what we have."

I force myself to say my worst fear. "Lexi wants the three of you to be a family, as in two parents living together with their child. I can tell."

"But that's not what I want. She's suggested we get back together a few times, using Nora as an excuse. But there's no way I can forgive her for what she took from me. I missed out on *two years* of my daughter's life."

I take in his sincere expression, and something in me relaxes. I'm not getting in the way of a family here. He's not in love with Lexi.

He continues, "I also wanted you to know that Lexi and Nora are moving to Summerdale. I can see Nora every Sunday this way, and I hope more."

My jaw drops, and I snap it shut. "Wow. Were you expecting that?"

He runs a hand over his face. "You've seen how Lexi operates, copying my key and popping in on us, surprising me on Father's Day to announce I'm a father. Of course, I didn't know. She's cut out of her snooty mom social circle because Nora didn't get into one of the private preschools in the city, so Lexi's starting over here."

"Because you're here."

"That and because we have good public schools."

My mind sorts through all the facts as I try to figure out how I feel.

"I care about you, Eve." He strokes my hair back from my face and cradles my cheek. I can feel my defenses crumbling. "Please don't shut me out over this."

"I don't want to get hurt," I whisper.

"You won't." He kisses my temple, my cheek, my jaw. His words are hot against my sensitive ear. "Everything between us will be open and honest from here on out. Only what you're comfortable with."

I pull back to look at him, teetering on the edge of reason and emotion.

His blue eyes are warm on mine and tender, so tender. He frames my face in his hands, lowering his head slowly until his lips meet mine. The rush of sensation at contact, the overwhelming sense of rightness decides for me. I surrender to it, reveling in the feel of his velvety lips, his taste, his scent.

He pulls away, his fingers lingering for one last caress, trailing along my jawline to the line of my neck. A shiver runs through me. "Let me take you home."

I nod and rise on shaky legs. I don't know where this is heading, but I want to find out. I'm ready for something real.

13

Dominic

I pull up to Jenna and Eli's house to pick up Eve for dinner, our first real date. I'm jittery with nerves like a teenager. I know it's ridiculous at my age and with my experience. It's just that Eve is different. Special. Emotions I thought were long buried are coming up again—hope for a future, longing, intense lust. Ha. We did this a bit backward in that department, but I'm going to try to slow things down enough for us to get to know each other.

I ring the bell, rocking back and forth on my heels.

Jenna answers, her green eyes bright with mischief. "Dr. Russo, I didn't know you made house calls!" Her dogs, Mocha and Lucy, rush forward to greet me. After a brief bark, they both sniff me loudly. I'm sure they recognize me. I took care of Mocha before he was adopted, and I've seen both of them for checkups since then.

Jenna steps back, inviting me in. "Eve's getting ready. She's changed outfits four times already."

I hide a smile. Maybe Eve's taking this as seriously as I am. Mocha, a brown pit bull, nudges my hand for pets. I rub his side.

"Hey, Dominic," Eli says, appearing from the kitchen with

the baby held against his chest. Theo looks cozy in a green blanket sleeper with a matching cap.

"Hey." I approach them. "And how's the little guy?"

Theo lifts his head from his dad's shoulder to stare at me.

I smile. "Hi. You look like you're about to fall asleep."

Eli smiles down at him. "It's never that easy. Theo requires movement. We either have to walk until we collapse or take him on a car ride."

"Once he's walking, he'll probably be on the move constantly."

Jenna smacks her forehead. "I hadn't even thought of that. We've got it easy now."

"I wouldn't say easy," Eli says.

Eve appears, walking downstairs toward us in a hurry. "Sorry to make you wait."

My mouth goes dry. She's so beautiful. Her blond hair has streaks of honey color, and the short cut accentuates her high cheekbones, blue eyes, and lush lips. And she has just the right amount of curves.

"You're worth the wait," I say hoarsely.

Her lips part, her eyes dilating.

"Wow," Jenna says. "Some serious chemistry going on here. Go on, you two. Have fun tonight. Don't rush home on my account. Eli and I can manage one night on our own with our demanding spawn."

Eli chuckles. "I hope we can manage more than one night on our own since we've got about eighteen years ahead of us."

"Don't worry, he'll be much easier to manage as a teen," Eve says with a wicked smile. "Not."

I wave bye and guide Eve out the door. We head to my car, and I open the passenger-side door for her. "You look beautiful," I tell her.

A faint pink color dots her cheeks. "Thanks."

She gets in, and I shut the door, taking a few deep breaths on my way to the driver's side. Somehow tonight feels like a test to see if we have a future.

As soon as I start the car, she says, "I didn't really change my outfit four times. Jenna was teasing."

"I'd feel better if you had, then I wouldn't feel awkward about changing twice."

"You did?" she asks softly.

I pinch her chin and kiss her. "I want everything to be perfect for you tonight."

"So where are we headed?"

"Happy Endings in Clover Park just over the border in Connecticut. It's a restaurant and bar, and in the back, they have a dance floor, jukeboxes, and pool tables. It looks fun. I've only been to the bar."

"I know that place."

I pull out of the driveway and head in the direction of Route 15. "So you've been there?"

"When I was a kid, it was Garner's Sports Bar and Grill. The back room is new. My family and I used to get brunch there, and then, after the divorce, just me and Dad would go there for dinner sometimes. We lived in a condo in Eastman, the town next door to Clover Park."

"In the spirit of openness, Audrey invited me for drinks at the bar there, which in retrospect seems odd since she told me she goes to The Horseman Inn bar for ladies' night every week and meets up with her friends there regularly."

"She wanted you all to yourself."

"Or she didn't want anyone to see us together."

"I'm beginning to think we don't need so much openness. Like, I'd rather not hear about your previous dates with women I know or don't know."

"Fair enough, but I'd like to know all about your history."

She tilts her head to the side, her eyes twinkling. "Well, there was Ron, who had a foot fetish. I had to draw the line at—"

"Yeah, hold it right there. I don't need to know the sexual proclivities of past men. Just, well, besides your ex-husband, was there anyone serious?"

"Let's just say I desperately wanted to stay together with

the men in my life, and they could take or leave me, and they usually left. I know that's more a reflection of where I was at during that point in my life and the poor choices I made. I've had years of therapy to get my self-esteem to a place where I make better choices. Until I finally decided single life suited me better than the upheaval of emotions every time I tried to connect with someone. And then I met you, and here we are."

I slow to a stop before merging onto Route 15 and give her a sympathetic look.

She stares straight ahead. "I've said too much."

"No, I'm glad you did. We've both been through some stuff, but that's history. We don't need to talk about it if you don't want to."

"I really don't."

"No problem. Tell me about your work. It sounds fascinating."

That gets her talking. And she's funny as hell describing the writers' room and the oddities of her coworkers, including one guy's pet iguana, which he can't stop talking about, and another writer who needs to lie down to brainstorm and frequently does so in the center of their conference room table.

Before I know it, we're in Clover Park. Unlike Summerdale, which is laid out like a wheel with the lake at the hub of town, Clover Park is on a neat grid with Main Street running down the center with side roads of the grid leading to houses, churches, and schools. I pull into the parking lot behind the restaurant, walk around, and open her door for her.

"Did your mom teach you to open doors for women?" she asks. "It's a dying art."

"My dad did. Some women appreciate it; some hate it. Where do you stand?"

She smiles up at me. "I like it. It feels like you're making the extra effort for my comfort."

"That's exactly right."

It's already dark now that it's the second week of October

with a nip in the air. Eve shivers. "I should've brought a jacket. I'm not used to this weather anymore."

"Wish I had one to give you."

We hurry around the side of the building, and I open the front door for her. We step into what looks like someone's birthday party. There's "Happy Birthday" balloons, as well as streamers, around the perimeter of the ceiling, at each table in the dining room, and at the hostess stand. Everyone in the dining room has a slice of birthday cake in front of them. It's difficult to hear the hostess greet us over the chatter of the crowd.

"Is this a private party?" I ask.

The hostess, a young brunette, smiles. "Nope. It's Maggie O'Hare's half birthday. She likes to celebrate here in hopes of lots of people joining in. Ninety-one and a half and still going strong."

"Does she always celebrate her half birthdays?" Eve asks.

"Once she turned ninety, she decided a year was too long to wait to celebrate. It's just an excuse for a party."

"She sounds like a fun lady," Eve says.

The hostess nods. "You'll probably see her dance the tango later with her husband, Jorge. It's mostly her grandkids and great-grandkids here, but they only took over the two long tables in back. You can sit anywhere you like, or if you want more quiet, try the bar."

I glance at Eve. "Bar?"

She nods.

Just then the birthday girl stands up. Maggie's a white-haired lady wearing a tiara and a leopard-print leotard with a fluffy pink skirt. "Since it's my half birthday, I'm the one giving out presents," she announces. "Everyone gets a free dance lesson at Jorge's dance studio."

There's a collective groan from the crowd.

"You always give us that," one teenaged girl complains.

"You just want to make us dance," a boy says.

Maggie gestures grandly. "Whoever wants to miss out on this great present should prove to me what a good dancer they are. Back room, everyone!" She gestures to an older man with black and gray hair to join her. I'm guessing it's Jorge from the way he looks at her. They lead off a conga line to the back room.

I check in with Eve in case she wants to sit in the main dining room, but she points to the bar. "They'll be back," she says.

We head over to the bar and take a couple of empty seats near the end. There's a good crowd here, too, with a group of ladies clustered together, laughing like old friends.

One of them lifts her glass, "To the Happy Endings Book Club!"

"At Happy Endings!" another says.

"I had a much better name for the club," another says. She has red hair and a hawk tattoo on her chest, showing through the skinny straps of a black tank top.

A stunning blonde woman with long hair and a formfitting pink dress huffs. "Mad, no one wanted to be called SLITS."

"Oh, really, Princess Hailey. Well, I wouldn't say that HEBC rolls off the tongue. Not like slits." She darts her tongue out.

The women crack up before clinking glasses and drinking.

I lean close to Eve's ear and whisper, "Do you want to go somewhere quieter?"

"Are you kidding me? This is eavesdropping gold for a writer. I collect dialogue and quirky personality traits everywhere I go."

"Really? So I could show up as a character in *Irreverent*?"

She smiles mysteriously.

"The dashing veterinarian with the awesome muscle car. People would definitely tune in for that."

"Honestly, I never use one person. It's a combination of traits all mushed together."

"Oh."

She nudges my shoulder with hers. "But I personally am enjoying the dashing vet with the muscle car."

"And I'm enjoying the beautiful writer with a heart of gold."

She puts a hand on her heart, blinking a few times. "You think I have a heart of gold? I've been told I'm closed off, cold even."

I cradle her jaw, stroking her cheek with my thumb. "Not the Eve I know."

Our gazes lock. I'm not sure who moves first, but the next thing I know, we're kissing passionately. I've never been drawn into a kiss the way she pulls me in, like a drowning man needing more and more.

She pulls away suddenly, putting her hand on my chest as if to hold me off. "We should order food and do date-like things."

"What do you usually do on a date?"

She gives me an impish smile, rubbing my chest. "I let men adore me and say flattering things all night long."

"Hmm, let me think up some good stuff to say."

"You have to think about it?" she says in mock outrage.

I smile. "What other brilliant things have you written? Have you ever done a movie?"

"Actually, I'm working on a screenplay about a fantasy world called Nadirr. I've had a couple of scripts optioned, but so far none have been made. It takes a long time to get something turned into a film, if ever. I've been trying for the last seven years."

"So TV writing pays the bills while you try to get a movie made."

"Actually, I like both."

"That's great to like your work."

"I love it."

I think but don't say, then it seems like you're in the right place, living in LA. I don't want to ruin the moment by bringing up what will ultimately separate us.

A voice carries over from the crowd of women. "It's those hell-on-wheels Campbell genes. Don't worry, he'll settle down in about twenty years."

More laughter from the ladies and a groan.

Eve pulls a small notepad from her purse. "I've got to write this stuff down!"

~

Eve

I'm still smiling about last night as I shower at Dominic's place late the next morning. Not only was dinner with Dominic so relaxed and fun, we had a great time afterward dancing with the birthday party people and the hilarious women from the bar. We went back to his place, where Dominic indulged me by watching more *Irreverent*, which he says is his new favorite show. It reminded me of how much I miss work. Unfortunately, the negotiations aren't going well. Some of the writers' grievances were leaked to the press with counter-responses from the producers' association. It's never good when it gets into a press battle for who's right in the public eye. The only good thing is I get to extend my stay in Summerdale.

There's so much for me here. I'm bonding with my baby nephew, starting fresh with Mom (we had lunch again this week), enjoying time with my sister and brother-in-law, meeting all sorts of nice people, and, for the first time ever, forging a deep connection with a good man. Before I was afraid to go for a relationship, but seeing Jenna and Eli's example up close, moving past the hurt over Mom's abandonment, getting to know Dominic and letting him get to know me, all of it allowed me to be open for more.

I've never been so happy. Yet, it's all temporary. My real life with my dream career is three thousand miles away.

I turn off the shower, grab a towel on a nearby hook, and dry off briskly, pushing down the angst over the future. It's the only way to enjoy the now, and now is really awesome. I clear the condensation from the bathroom mirror. My face is glowing with happiness. Oh, I have beard burn on the side of my neck. Dominic's five-o'clock shadow comes in around three. Ha-ha. We can't keep our hands off each other.

I sigh as I pull on one of Dominic's old T-shirts. I actually feel like I'm floating. I brush my teeth with the toothbrush he gave me and walk back to the bedroom to finish getting dressed in yesterday's clothes with fresh underwear I packed in my purse. Hey, I never expected to be able to resist him after our date.

PJ lifts his head, giving me a tired look from his fleece bed next to Dominic's bed. He has another little bed in the living room and moves from one to the other according to his moods. Mostly he sleeps. He never barks or whines, merely accepts life as it comes. He's almost like a cat.

"You can go back to sleep," I tell him.

I sit on the edge of the mattress to put my socks and shoes on. Dominic went to work for his Saturday morning shift while I slept in. I know he puts in some time at the animal shelter on Saturday afternoons too. Jenna encouraged me to fill in for a few Saturday afternoon shifts, so I thought I'd join him later. She'll often walk the dogs and do whatever else needs doing. Hopefully, he doesn't object to spending more time together. It's just that I don't know how long I'll be here, so I kinda want to soak in all the happiness I can get.

PJ's head lifts, his black pointy ears perking up as the front door opens.

I go to the living room. "Hi!" I'm both excited to see Dominic and what he's carrying—coffee and a Summerdale Sweets pastry box. I love all of my sister's recipes.

"Good morning, sunshine. I brought a late breakfast."

"You just get more and more awesome."

He smiles widely. "Is that so?" He sets the coffee and box down on the kitchen counter. He turns to face me, and I throw myself into his arms, hugging him around the middle.

He holds me for a moment before leaning back, his large hand stroking the side of my face. "I didn't know you had a sweet side."

I can't help my smile. "I'm just happy. I had a great time

last night, and I'm happy to see you today. Do you mind if I join you at the animal shelter this afternoon? Jenna wanted me to take her place at least once to help out."

He kisses me. "That sounds great."

I bounce a little on the balls of my feet. "Great!" I turn to the pastry box and open it. Mmm, blueberry and raspberry muffins with crumb topping. "I think I'm in love."

"What?"

I grab a muffin and take a bite. "With these." I chew and swallow. "To die for. Thank you." My emotions are showing. *I think I'm in love.* I said it about muffins, but part of me meant it toward him.

He searches my expression. "Gotta feed you."

I take a sip of coffee. "PJ missed you when you were gone."

He boxes me in against the counter, his eyes alight with mischief. "Did he?"

I nod, the blood rushing through my veins. He lifts me to the counter, fitting himself between my legs. "I missed him too."

I set my breakfast on the counter and wrap my arms around his neck. "Dominic." One word that's come to mean so much. I don't know how I'm going to walk away from this.

And then his mouth's on mine, his palm sliding down my spine to my bottom, pressing me harder against him. That delicious point of contact sends a rush of desire through me.

"Take me," I say between kisses.

He pulls my clothes off, somehow barely breaking the kiss as he goes. He turns me suddenly, bending me over the counter.

Desire wars with nagging worry. I haven't forgotten how Lexi barged in with Nora. "Wait. We're out in the open."

His fingers slide between my legs, stroking in teasing circles. "So?"

"What if your ex lets herself in?"

He kisses and bites gently along the side of my neck as his

fingers continue their torture. He tugs my earlobe between his teeth. "I changed the locks."

My limbs go weak as the last of my defenses crumble. I hear the rustle of a condom wrapper, and then he grabs my hips, holding me steady, and thrusts inside. I gasp as he fills me to the hilt.

He whispers in my ear, "You're so sexy. I'm going to make you come now."

My breath shudders out, knowing he'll make good on that sexy promise. He takes me in slow deep thrusts as he caresses and strokes, giving me just what I need. Passion has never been so overwhelming. My mind goes blank, and I completely let go, surrendering to all he can give.

He whispers praise in my ear, "Yes, just like that."

A haze of sensation carries me away, and then he hits just the right spot, and I go off in an explosion that rocks me to my core, sensations radiating in wave after wave. He yanks me hard against him as he lets go with a guttural groan.

His breath is harsh by my ear. "I can't get enough of you."

My heart sinks. "Me too." It's going to be so hard to say goodbye. I wish I could stop thinking about the future, but it's just staring at me like a big FADE OUT—beautiful Summerdale movie over.

He turns me to face him, cupping my face in his warm hands. "What's wrong?"

"Nothing."

"Eve, tell me. You sound sad. I thought you'd be jubilant like you were before we had sex. I thought it was last night's sex that made you that way."

It's you. I hug him tight, resting my cheek against his chest, listening to the steady beat of his heart. "I've just never been so happy, and it scares me because I know it won't last with the long distance."

"We'll figure something out."

"But you're tied here, and I'm tied—" His mouth covers mine, kissing the protest from my lips. The kiss is tender, loving even, his body conveying what words could never do. The emotion is real, and it's not one-sided.

He pulls back, resting his forehead against mine. We share a breath and then another, bound together for a timeless moment.

The clank of metal hitting the floor grabs our attention. I look over. PJ just dropped his leash at our feet. He lifts big eyes from me to Dominic and back. He wants to go outside.

Dominic chuckles. "I'll take you."

I take a bite of delicious raspberry muffin. I could get used to this.

When we arrive at the shelter, I'm surprised to find Audrey and Drew already there. They're in the cat room, where Audrey is pointing out the different cats to Drew.

Dominic knocks on the glass and waves at them. Audrey steps out, Drew close behind her.

"Wow," Audrey says. "Looks like you've got a lot of extra hands today. Hi, Eve, did you two come in together?"

I point to the door we just walked through. "Right through that door."

She studies me for a moment and seems to see something that tells her we're together. Oh, God, do I have that *just had sex* look? I splashed cold water on my face before we left. Maybe it's the beard burn on my neck. I put my hand there, covering it up.

Dominic offers Drew his hand, and they exchange a firm handshake. "Audrey invited you too. That's great."

Audrey's blue eyes dance with barely concealed glee. "He's the newest member of book club, and we got to talking afterward about how rewarding it is to spend time at the shelter, and *voila*!"

"I like dogs," Drew mutters.

"He had some time after the kids' karate classes finished," Audrey adds. She tries not to smile, but can't manage it.

I stifle a laugh. Seems Audrey's pleased to have Drew tagging along to her favorite activities.

Dominic rubs his hands together. "I'm glad to have you both here. Eve and I will go through with meals for the dogs. If you could replenish water as needed, and then I'll need help taking the dogs out for a walk. You can take them two at a time. Any more than that and they get too excited, which is never good after a meal."

Dominic and I go toward a back room, where he keeps the dog food. As we're walking away, I hear Audrey say, "They seem like they're a couple, right?"

Drew replies in such a low voice I can't overhear. Darn it.

I want to say, "Yes! We're a couple," but something stops me from saying it out loud. In my heart, we're together. Somehow saying it out loud means the happy spell will be broken. There's too much uncertainty about the future, too many questions I don't know the answer to.

14

Eve

I meet Mom at The Horseman Inn for lunch. It's our third mother-daughter lunch, and I feel a lot more comfortable being with her just the two of us. I guess it took her diagnosis for me to push past my hurt and connect with her again, and maybe that made her more willing to ask for forgiveness too.

This is our second time in a row at The Horseman Inn. I think she likes running into people she knew in town before she moved away. We're here on a Tuesday instead of our usual Wednesday lunch because her surgery is on Thursday morning, and she didn't think she'd be up to eating much the day before since she'd be so nervous.

I take a seat, and a smiling Mom sits across from me, waving to the owner of the restaurant. "So good to see you again, Sydney!"

Sydney smiles serenely. "Good to have you and Eve back in town." I'm never one to say a woman needs a man to make her life complete, but it's obvious that marriage and mother-hood agree with Sydney. She used to be a bundle of bristling energy. A bit aggressive too, punching people on the shoulder when she liked them.

"We'll have to get Theo and little Quinn together for a playdate," Mom says.

"I'm sure we will," Sydney says. "Enjoy your lunch."

Just then, a tall guy with tousled brown hair and scruff on his jaw walks in with a squalling baby wearing a white bonnet and purple dress. He rushes to Sydney. "I tried to calm her down, but she only wants milkies."

Sydney gestures to him. "My husband, Wyatt, and our devil child, Quinn."

Wyatt thrusts the baby into her arms and turns to us. "That's an inside joke because we call each other the devil in a loving way."

"I'm sure she's very sweet," Mom says as Quinn lets out a full-throttle wail that vibrates my eardrums.

Sydney sighs. "Let's go, Quinn, and then I really have to work. I can't strap you on all day."

"Actually…" Wyatt follows her with a baby Bjorn.

Mom and I exchange a look of baby understanding.

"Theo's a much easier baby," Mom whispers.

"He never screams like that." Though, to be fair, he sure can fuss a lot.

"I'm so happy I get to be a grandmother," Mom says.

"Thank Jenna."

"What about you, Eve?" she asks gently. "Is that something you'd like in your future?"

My lips part. I never used to think so, but lately the idea has real appeal. Still, my future is so uncertain, I'm not sure how to answer. We're interrupted by the waitress setting down glasses of water and giving us menus.

Mom beams at our waitress, the same woman from when I was here with Dominic. "Ellen, hi! It's Meghan Larsen."

They get into a lively conversation. Seems Mom knows everyone in town and loves being here. She moved away after Jenna graduated college because she felt too alone in her house. She sold it and moved to an apartment closer to her work. Now she works part-time from home in the condo she shares with Dad. Mom's in computer work. I don't quite understand it. Jenna used to do similar until she burned out and decided to move back to Summerdale to open a bakery. I didn't inherit that analytical gene. I give Mom a lot of credit for going back to college after she had me and Jenna. I'm sure it wasn't easy.

After the waitress leaves, I venture to ask the question I've been wondering about ever since Mom told me her diagnosis. "Are you okay about the surgery?"

"I am. Today, anyway. Don't ask me tomorrow. I've only ever had surgery to take out my wisdom teeth before."

"Any surgery is scary. I'll be there for you. So will Jenna, Eli, and Dad. Theo will be having fun with his uncle Caleb and aunt Sloane. They want practice with a baby before theirs comes along." I smile, trying to sound normal like I'm not terrified I'm going to lose Mom just when we finally reconnected.

She reaches across the table and takes my hand in hers. She's quiet for a moment, looking down. When she finally meets my eyes, hers are teary. "Eve, I can't tell you how much it's meant to me to have these mother-daughter lunches with you. I always hoped—" Her voice chokes on a sob.

"Mom, it's okay." I fumble for a tissue in my purse, my own eyes welling. I can't let myself fall apart before her surgery; then she'll know how worried I am. I hand her a tissue.

She wipes her tears and takes a quivery breath. "I promised myself I wouldn't get too emotional."

"It's okay."

"You're more like him, you know. Your dad."

"I know." Dad worked his way up to manager in a super-market, but he's a secret poet, always searching for the perfect word or phrase.

"It's why I thought it made sense that you chose him when the judge asked you, and deep down I knew you'd probably be better off with him."

"Mom, I'm okay. Really. I've worked through all this in therapy. You've apologized more than once. We don't have to rehash it. I've forgiven you. I want us to move forward."

She nods, biting her lip. "I want that too."

I change the subject, telling her the latest in the strike negotiations. I've never been so torn over the email updates on the situation. Part of me is discouraged that the strike is dragging on because that means no work, and part of me is relieved I don't have to leave Summerdale yet.

I glance over as a dark-haired toddler rushes by our table, heading to the back dining room. Her mom follows at a quick pace. "Nora, I told you not to run ahead without Mommy. This is not a playground."

Shit. It's Dominic's ex-wife. I pull the menu up, hiding my face. The last thing I want is to deal with her. I haven't spent any time with Nora either because Dominic doesn't want her to get attached to me. At first I was hurt when he told me that. I understand, though. I'm leaving.

I watch as Nora climbs up to a chair and takes the napkin from the table, putting it on her lap, and looking at her mom expectantly.

"Good girl," her mom says.

Nora beams. Her bright smile reminds me of her dad's, the way it lights their eyes up. His eyes sparkle, sometimes with amusement, sometimes with sexy mischief.

"Do you know them?" Mom asks me.

I blink a few times, snapping back to attention. "Not really."

"The little girl is adorable." Mom turns and waves at her. Nora waves back.

"Mom, don't do that! Don't attract attention."

She turns back to me. "What's wrong?"

"Nothing. Just don't wave to her."

Ellen returns to take our order. When she leaves, Mom studies me for a long moment and seems to choose her words carefully. "Jenna told me you've been seeing someone in town, a single dad."

"You and Jenna talk about me?"

"Not usually, but I happened to mention how I wish you'd stay in Summerdale and—"

"You do?"

"Of course I do. So does your dad and Jenna, and I'm sure if baby Theo could talk, he'd say the same. I didn't say anything because I know it has to be your decision. It's your life. It's selfish of me to want you close to make up for lost time. That's not your responsibility."

I glance over as Nora gets a plastic cup with a straw and takes a big sip. "I guess not."

"Jenna hoped your single dad might make you want to stay."

I stiffen. "I'm not giving up my job for any man. It's not easy to get into the writers' room of a hit show. I was just promoted to story editor. I could get a producer credit next season. I'd be crazy to leave it behind for the possibility of a happy ending. I don't believe in those, Jenna being the exception."

My chest tightens. Everything I said is the painful truth. And I don't like Jenna and Mom discounting the importance of my career. They're doing what they want to do for work. We all make life choices.

My eye catches on Nora talking animatedly, her eyes bright and happy. Lexi's listening and nodding. I'm glad to see that.

Mom glances at the back dining room. "Is that his daughter you can't take your eyes off of?"

I shift uncomfortably in my seat. I hadn't realized it, but I guess I was checking on Nora. She's coloring a kids' menu now, very intent on her task while her mom looks at her phone. "Yes. I've only met her once, so she might not remember me." *Actually, twice, but I hid under the covers most of that first time.* "I don't want to deal with her mom."

"Is she as angelic as she looks? The girl, I mean."

I can't afford to get attached to Nora, angelic or not. "Her dad makes her sound like an angel. I'm sure she has her faults."

"Don't we all?"

∾

After we finished lunch, we sat at the table for a long time talking. Mom asked me a lot of questions about my job and how things worked in Hollywood for a writer. I appreciated her taking me and my work seriously. Now we're in the parking lot to say bye.

Mom's eyes tear up. "I so enjoy our time together." She hugs me and doesn't let go.

My throat tightens. It almost feels like a final goodbye.

She pulls back and cups my face. "I know your work is important to you, but I also wish for you what your sister has, a loving husband and a child to love."

"Why not throw in a couple of dogs too?" I ask sarcastically. "I'll just take over Jenna's life, and the transformation will be complete. The daughter you always wanted."

She looks deep into my eyes. "I love you. I always have. I always will."

My composed facade breaks, and a tear escapes. "Mom, don't say that like we're saying goodbye."

"I just want to let those I love know how I feel."

"You're going to be okay. This is a blip, like you said."

She pats my cheek. "I'm sure you're right. All the same, I love you."

My chest aches fiercely. The words feel like they're wrenched from a dark sheltered place deep from within. "I love you too."

She gives me a watery smile before heading for her car.

And I just stand there in the parking lot, feeling like a lost little girl. She's going to die and leave me again.

I shake my head at myself. No, she's *scared* she's going to die. That's why it feels like goodbye. She'll make it through this. She has to.

≈

Jenna and I hold vigil in the Eastman Hospital waiting room during Mom's surgery. Dad went to get coffee in the cafeteria with Eli, and Theo is with Eli's brother Caleb and his wife, Sloane.

"We should've heard something by now," I whisper to Jenna.

She's been working her way through a pack of cherry Twizzlers, chewing ferociously. "I know. Should we ask someone?"

"I'm sure they'd tell us if something was wrong."

She chomps on another Twizzler. "Yesterday she stopped by to tell me she loved me and hugged me for a really long time. It was almost like she knew this was it."

"Don't say that."

"It's true."

"She did the same with me," I admit. "She was just scared. She'll pull through."

Dad and Eli return with coffee for all of us. After they hand it out, they take the seats on either side of us, Dad by me, Eli by Jenna.

"Any news?" Dad asks.

"Not yet."

His leg bounces up and down. He sets the coffee on a side table. "I don't need this. I'm jittery enough as it is." He turns to me. "What's new with you?"

"Not much. Still on strike. Having a good time with Theo and fam," I say, giving Jenna's arm a squeeze on my other side.

Dr. Weitz appears in the waiting room and approaches us. She's in her fifties, so I like to think her experience is to our advantage. Dad leaps from his seat.

"She did well," Dr. Weitz says to Dad. Seeing us all hanging on every word, she speaks to us as a group. "No surprises. She's in the recovery room. Once she comes out of anesthesia, you can go see her."

Dad collapses to his chair. "Thank you, Dr. Weitz."

She nods. "A nurse will be out to tell you when you can see her." She turns and leaves.

Dad runs a shaky hand through his white blond hair. "I can't relax until I see her."

I lean my head against his shoulder. I know what he means. I'm anxious to see her too.

An hour of tense conversation, four Twizzlers, half a coffee, and horrifying images on the news channel playing on the waiting room's TV have me about to leap out of my skin.

"What's taking so long?" Jenna says. "I'm going to find out what's going on."

She marches over to the reception desk. Even from here we can hear her loudly demanding to see Mom. Eli goes to her side as backup. After a terse conversation with the guy behind the desk, they return to their seats.

"They're sending someone to check on her status," Eli says.

We all sit there on the edges of our seats. I want to cry, but I can't. Everything is bottled up inside, the not-knowing, the fear, the only recently found connection with Mom. I can't lose her. I won't lose her.

A young nurse appears a few minutes later, her hands clasped tightly in front of her. "Hi, I'm Melissa. I just checked on Meghan, and she's taking a little longer to come out of anesthesia than expected, but don't worry. Sometimes that happens. Has she ever had a reaction to anesthesia before?"

"I don't think she's had anesthesia before," Dad says.

"She told me she had her wisdom teeth out," I say. "She didn't mention anything about a reaction to anesthesia."

"Okay, we'll keep monitoring her and let you know. Like I said, try not to worry. Everyone responds differently to anesthesia."

She turns and walks briskly back through the double doors that shut us away from Mom.

Dad crumples, dropping his head in his hands. Even after their hellish divorce, they still love each other. I catch Jenna's eye, and she gestures to switch seats with her. I stand, and she takes my seat, putting an arm around Dad. Eli sits next to her in silent support.

I drop into the seat across from them, misery a tight band around my chest. I can barely get a breath. I pull my phone out, wanting to text Dominic, but then I don't know what to say. I want him here for comfort, but I don't have the right to ask him that. We're not in a committed relationship. Not like Jenna and Eli.

I glance back toward reception, and my breath catches at a familiar confident stride heading right toward me. Dominic.

He showed up when I needed him.

15

My last defense crumbles. I love this man. He showed up when I needed him most, and not for the first time. He was there when I found an injured dog, when my tire went flat, he went to karate class to make up with me, and he was at the bar that very first night we met just like he said he'd be. This is a man I can trust, one I can depend on. Emotion clogs my throat. Love isn't how I expected it to feel. It was a slow inevitable slide, and now that I'm in it, I can barely speak.

I rush toward him. He wraps his arms around me without a word. I sag against him, soaking in the comfort of his strong, steady presence.

After a few moments, I pull back to look at him. "What're you doing here? I thought you had work."

"I rearranged my schedule to be here for you."

My eyes well. "You remembered today was the day."

"Of course I did."

"You don't have to be here," I manage to say over the lump in my throat.

He cups the side of my face. "I want to be. Is she out of surgery?"

"Yes, but she's taking longer than expected to regain consciousness after the anesthesia." My voice cracks. He wraps me in his arms, holding me close.

"Come on, let's have a seat," he murmurs. "Have you had anything to eat or drink?"

"Just Twizzlers and coffee."

"I'll get you some water." He guides me toward the chairs where my family sits. "Anything else you want?"

"Just you. Don't leave me."

"Okay."

I love you.

We sit across from my family.

"Hey, everyone," he says in a subdued tone. "I understand it's a waiting game. I'm sure she'll be fine. She's a strong woman."

"Thanks," Dad says.

Jenna nods and rests her head against Eli's shoulder.

"You don't know that she'll be fine," I whisper to him.

"She produced two strong women; of course she'd have to be strong too."

I blink back tears. Part of me feels like crying will bring bad luck. I have to believe everything will be all right.

He takes my hand in his, entwining our fingers together. A tear escapes. Every bad choice I made with past relationships stands in stark contrast to the way Dominic treats me. He respects me, cares for me. He's there for me. A true friend.

Forty-five terrifying minutes later, the nurse returns. "She's awake. You can go see her. One at a time, please."

Dad leaps up with a cheer, and suddenly we're all hugging in one big group hug. Jenna's laughing and crying at the same time, and that makes me cry.

"Who's first?" the nurse asks.

"Do one of you girls want to go first?" Dad asks.

"You go, Dad," Jenna says.

I nod. We both saw how he crumbled.

He leaves with the nurse.

"I thought your parents were divorced," Dominic says.

"Not in their hearts," I say. "They live together now."

"Ah."

I wrap my arms around his waist. "I want to see you again tomorrow. Can we do another date night?"

"Date night plus the next day like last weekend. I like having you over for as long as possible."

I turn to Jenna, about to ask if she can spare me or if she needs help with Theo, when she says with a big smile, "I'd never let Theo get in the way of true love."

I flush, speechless. I can't deny it.

Dominic looks equally flustered. "I, uh, we haven't…" He turns to me as if I have the answer.

"Thanks, Jenna," I say. "Dominic's become important to me."

He smiles widely, his eyes warm on mine. "You too."

Jenna claps. "Yes! I knew it!"

~

Dominic

Eve seems less guarded than before. She smiled a lot at dinner. Now we're back at my place, and she has PJ in her lap on the living room sofa, cooing to him and stroking him gently over his bony forehead and behind the ears.

"You seem different," I say, sitting next to her.

PJ gives me a baleful glare like he's afraid I'm going to steal Eve's attention. He's not wrong.

"Different how?" Eve asks.

"I don't know. Looser. More relaxed."

She gives me a soft smile. "Well, Mom's doing well, and I'm enjoying my time in Summerdale. Mostly because of you."

"Not Theo?" I tease.

She laughs. "Theo too, of course. He's always number one. But you're close. Right up there."

Warmth spreads through my chest. Something's definitely changed between us. She's more open to being with me. It makes me want to let my guard down too. "Everything seems brighter with you in my life."

She smiles and then gets serious. "I should tell you…"

"What?"

She focuses on PJ, stroking him gently. "In the past, I've had bad relationships. Just choosing people who weren't great for me, drinking too much, drugs, not valuing myself enough. I got in a car accident because I was driving while high. Fortunately, I hit a telephone pole, and the only person I hurt was myself. I'm still trying to forgive myself for that. When I think of what could've happened, how much worse it could've been—"

"But nothing else did happen. Don't torture yourself over what-ifs in the past. You're okay now."

She stares at me, unblinking. "That's why I needed knee surgery. The accident that was my own stupid fault. And then I became addicted to painkillers. Next was my terrible choice to get married to my drug dealer followed by a divorce. I need you to know what kind of baggage you're dealing with here."

"I can only imagine how hard that must've been for you."

"Yes, well," she says uncertainly. "That doesn't concern you?"

"You're good now, aren't you?"

"After years of therapy, yes. I'm drug-free and avoid toxic men at all costs. Both are a kind of drug, with all the drama and wrenching emotions. It was like I was working through my shit in real time with other people, who weren't helping me move forward at all. I was stuck. I dropped toxic men, but haven't really let in any man. With you, I want to try."

A rush of affection has me shifting PJ out of the way and hauling her into my lap. PJ grunts his displeasure, but settles down quickly.

"Eve, thank you for sharing that with me. I get that it wasn't easy."

She runs her fingers through the hair at the nape of my neck. "You don't seem put off by it."

"It's behind you now. You did the hard work to heal, which shows great courage. I'm proud of you."

She blinks rapidly. "I worried you might think less of me."

"Never."

She kisses me tenderly, and a rush of lust and love race through me. And now I'm the one who needs to show courage because I'm in love and I have to find a way to make this work.

~

Eve

Dominic and I have a nice weekend thing going for the third week in a row. Sometimes I can't quite believe how fantastic things are going for us. There're no more secrets, and, most importantly, there's trust. That's a big one for me. Anyway, I've been spending the night on Friday nights, and the next day I join him at the shelter to help with the animals. I can see why Jenna loves to volunteer with the shelter. There's something so rewarding about taking care of the dogs and cats, knowing we're helping them feel comfortable in their temporary home before they find their forever home. Drew and Audrey have been there every Saturday afternoon too and seem to have a good partnership as they work together, trading off tasks efficiently. I even saw Drew crack a smile. Twice!

Now we're heading back to Dominic's place late Saturday afternoon. I've got about an hour and a half before I need to go to Jenna's house for family dinner. Mom's home from the hospital and is eager to see Theo again. It's been nine days since her surgery, and her recovery is going well.

When we get back to Dominic's place, I take PJ out to do his business, praise him lavishly, and bring him back inside. I love taking care of this disgruntled little Boston terrier. Dominic says his expression is more a matter of age and PJ's facial structure than actual haughtiness or disgruntlement. Still, I love his expressions. He reminds me of myself in my younger days. Never happy, trying to keep myself separate as the only defense I had, until I threw myself into a bad relationship. It was a lot of hot and cold, a lot of disasters. That's over. Now I'm in a good place in my life.

"It's nice out," I say. "We should take a walk around the lake."

PJ sends me a disturbed stare over his shoulder before settling in his fleece bed next to the sofa.

"You don't have to go," I tell PJ before turning to Dominic. "How about you?"

"I'm kinda beat. Do you mind if we hang here? The sofa's calling my name." He walks over and flops down on it. "I think it's calling your name too." He shifts to his side and pats the cushion next to him. Then out of the side of his mouth, he calls, "Eve, Eve."

I lie down on my side, throwing an arm and leg over him. "Your sofa impersonation is so convincing."

He strokes my hair back, his eyes intent on mine. "Keeping late nights with you and early morning appointments on Saturdays is rough. If this keeps up, I'll have to hire someone part-time. I can't cut back on my love life. You're irresistibly sexy."

I giggle, something I never used to do. "Stop. You'd do that for me?"

He kisses me. "I'd do anything for you."

My heart melts, emotions rushing through me, making me full to bursting with love. I want to tell him how I feel. But then his mouth's on mine, urgent and demanding, and desire takes over.

The doorbell rings, and we break apart.

"Are you expecting anyone?" I ask.

"No." He untangles himself from me and gets off the sofa. "Probably a Cub Scout selling popcorn. It's that time of year."

I relax. Good, I get more cuddle time. I've never been cuddled before Dominic. Of course, it doesn't always last long. Usually lust ignites within seconds, but then we cuddle again afterward. Sometimes we even fall asleep wrapped around each other.

"Hi, were you busy?" a woman's voice asks.

"Hi, Daddy!"

I jackknife upright and smooth my hair. Nora and Lexi, the woman I'm trying not to hate because she seems to take good care of Nora. I just hate what she did to Dominic.

"Hi, Nora!" he says as she rushes inside. She hugs his leg, and he ruffles her hair. So sweet. It seems Dominic has forged a connection with her since he's been able to see her every Sunday.

Lexi looks past him to me, gives me a blank look, and then turns back to him. "We're heading to the playground and wanted to see if you'd like to join us. There's one on the other side of the lake."

"Swing!" Nora says, tugging on the fabric of Dominic's jeans.

"You like swings?" Dominic asks.

Nora nods so hard her high ponytail hits her in the face. She shoves it back. "Slides too!"

"Slides too?" he asks in an excited voice. He glances back at me, a question in his eyes. He wants to go.

"Have fun," I say. "I was just heading out."

Dominic joins me, saying quietly, "Thanks for understanding. I'd invite you to join us, but we're not there yet, you know?"

I ignore the jab to my heart. He's said it before. Nora's had a lot of upheaval in her life, and he doesn't want her getting attached to me because we don't have a permanent thing. I'm only upset because I was actually starting to let myself imagine a future with him. I had this whole fantasy of being one of those bicoastal couples. I'd stay in LA during the *Irreverent* writing season and come back here to Summerdale off-season. He'd visit me on the weekends, and we'd make it work. My imagination should stick to script writing.

"We'll be outside," Lexi calls cheerfully.

The door shuts behind them.

The silence is charged between us. Dominic has another life without me, a whole family without me. I know that's what Lexi wants. I hate that he spends so much time with her.

I haven't said a word about it because of Nora. I would never let a child get hurt because of what an adult wants. That's me, the adult doing the adult thing.

I grab my purse. The words sound brittle to my ears, but I manage to get them out. "I'll see you on Tuesday at the Halloween party. Have fun with Nora."

He heaves a sigh. "Here I was thinking I'd get a little rest."

"Not with a toddler."

I give him a peck on the cheek and hurry out the door and down the stairs. Nora's squatting in the gravel parking lot, picking up rocks. Lexi smirks at me as I pass.

I don't say a word to either of them.

16

That night I help Jenna set the table for our take-out dinner with our parents.

"What's wrong?" Jenna asks. "You've seemed distant ever since you got back from Dominic's. Did you two have a fight?"

"No. It's nothing."

Eli walks in, carrying a sleeping Theo in his car seat. "I'm going to put him in his crib for a nap. I'll pick up the food next."

"He can't nap during dinner," Jenna says. "Mom's making a big effort to be here just to get her baby fill."

"An hour nap. By the time they get here, he'll be much more up for company."

She sighs and nods. Eli heads upstairs.

"Theo's been up since four a.m.," Jenna says. "We couldn't get him back to sleep until one this afternoon, and now his schedule's thrown off."

"Sorry. I should've been here to help."

She waves that away. "You have a right to a love life. How often does a guy like Dominic come along?"

I press my lips tightly together. Never. He's a once in a lifetime. But I don't belong in his little family. And the bicoastal thing was wishful thinking on my part, delusions brought on by my ridiculously happy state ever since he was there for me for Mom's surgery. I have to wonder if I purposely chose a man to love knowing it wouldn't last. A self-defense mechanism of sorts. I'm great at those.

She gestures for me to follow her to the kitchen, where she turns the faucet on warm. There's a few pots and pans in the sink.

"I'll get that," I say. "Go rest."

She sighs. "I can't rest. Mom and Dad will be here soon. Besides, I want to know what's going on with you."

I test the water and squirt some dish soap on a sponge. "You're very persistent."

"How often is my sister having a torrid love affair right under my nose?" She hops up on the counter and grins at me.

I focus on scrubbing a brownie pan. I thought I smelled chocolate when I came in. She probably baked it for tonight's dessert.

She pokes my arm.

"It's silly," I say.

"You know the extent of my flailing when Eli and I first got together. No judgment."

I shake my head. "I feel guilty even saying this because I have no place in this picture, and the last thing I want is for a child to be slighted in any way, it's just that Dominic left to go to the playground with Nora and Lexi. They came over while I was there. He didn't want to invite me because Nora's had upheaval in her life, losing her stepdad, moving, starting preschool, so he didn't want her to get attached to me in case I'm not a permanent part of her life. And I totally get that. I don't want to get attached to her for the same reason. Is this making any sense?"

"Absolutely. So Lexi and Nora just showed up unannounced?"

I rinse the pan, and Jenna holds her hand out for it, towel at the ready. "Yeah, they were on the way to the playground by the lake, so they stopped by."

Her eyes narrow. "I don't like Lexi at all. She must've seen your car out front. I think she's purposely trying to make you feel left out."

"It's not Dominic's fault she has no boundaries." I scrub a pot extra hard. Though he could set his foot down more. "Ex baggage, I get it."

"He has to draw the line."

"He's new at the dad thing." My eyes well, my shoulders drooping. I set the pot down and stare out the back window. "Getting in the middle feels wrong. They're a family."

"He's a single dad. You can still be with him. It's just more complicated."

"Maybe if I wasn't in the picture, Nora could have her parents together like a real family."

She shoots me a hard look. "You're imagining a future that will likely never happen. Would you ever take back a woman who hid your baby from you until her husband, whom she *cheated* on you with, died?"

I laugh a little because it sounds like a soap opera. "No."

"He's not stupid. He's never going to fall for Lexi again. I think he's just trying to make things easier for Nora. Don't read anything into that about yourself."

"But where do I fit?"

"With him."

I go back to washing the pot.

"And maybe one day with Nora too," she adds.

Every nerve ending stands on end. "Me, a stepmom?"

"Why not? You're great with Theo. Sometimes I think you're better at calming him than I am. And you're just as new at this." There's a catch in her voice.

I squeeze her arm. "You're great with him. It's easier for me because I don't have the mom hormones stressing me out every time he cries. I have just enough distance to stay calm. Things will smooth out for you."

She dashes away a tear. "Hormones are a bitch. Eli's as calm as ever."

"Would you really want to live with a man riding the hormonal roller coaster?"

Her eyes widen. "I shudder at the thought."

We crack up.

~

"Sit over here with him next to me," Mom says, patting the sofa.

Jenna takes Theo and sits next to Mom, who immediately starts cooing at him and putting her finger on his hand for him to grip.

"Mom, you're looking a little pale," Jenna says. "Maybe you'd like to lie down?"

"We could go home," Dad says.

"Not yet," Mom says. "I've been looking forward to this for days." She can't hold Theo since she's still recovering from surgery, so she's just been staying close to him.

"Eve, could you bring the brownies out with the dessert plates?" Jenna asks.

"Sure."

I head to the kitchen for the brownies in a large plastic container. Jenna's big on keeping baked goods fresh. The dogs bark suddenly, racing to the door, which sets Theo off on a wail.

I peek into the living room. Drew's here.

I set the brownies out on dessert plates on the dining room table. The room is just off the living room. "Dessert's ready!" I know better than to put any food on the living room coffee table. Mocha and Lucy will snarf them down immediately. Everyone knows chocolate is bad for dogs.

Drew appears first in the dining room. "Hey, Eve. No Dominic?"

"He's with his daughter."

"Ah. Is that weird for you?"

I'm surprised at his insight. From what Jenna told me, he's a clueless alpha. Though she may be biased because of the way he never made a move on her best friend, Audrey. "It's different."

"The key to dealing with kids is to talk to them like little adults."

"Is that right?"

"That's how I deal with my karate students. Makes them feel heard."

I stifle a laugh. Even with my limited experience with kids, that doesn't sound quite right. "Good to know."

My parents, Jenna, and Eli file into the room and sit down, conversation flowing freely about Theo and his amazing development. Jenna and Eli are proud parents, and the new grandparents hang on every word because they're just as proud.

Drew lifts his brows at me with an amused look. I smile back.

"Anyone want a drink?" I ask. A chorus of requests comes at me.

"Water."

"Milk would be great."

"Coffee."

A few more milks, and that's everyone. I memorize it quickly and go to the kitchen. I used to work as a waitress while I was struggling to get into a writers' room. That was before I finally got a gig as a writer's assistant, which gave me the foot in the door I needed.

By the time I've served everyone their drinks, Theo is starting to get fussy. Jenna nurses him.

As soon as I sit down, everyone starts eating brownies, except Drew, who's pushed his plate away. He probably doesn't eat any sweets. The man is super fit like the soldier he used to be. I'm sure all the karate helps too.

"Here I thought you showed up at this time for my dessert," Jenna teases Drew. Eli feeds her a bite of brownie.

"Sorry I couldn't make dinner," Drew says. "I was helping a friend move some stuff."

"Who?" Eli asks.

"Audrey's parents are getting ready to sell their house, and she wanted some of their furniture. A chaise lounge and a Stickley desk with a matching chair. Excellent workmanship on the desk."

"Isn't that nice of you to do a favor for a *friend*," Jenna says.

Drew looks at her stone-faced. "I'd do the same for anyone."

"Mmm-hmm," Jenna says. "I bet—" She's cut off by Eli feeding her more brownie.

I smile. Good timing. Jenna likes to needle Drew about Audrey because she's frustrated on Audrey's behalf. I say if it's going to happen, it probably would have by now. I think they must truly be friends. Just like Audrey and Dominic. And who couldn't use a good friend? Especially when Audrey's good friends are all married and busy with their babies now.

After the brownies are devoured, I clear the plates and load the dishwasher. I feel guilty for abandoning Jenna to spend half my weekend with Dominic.

My nephew lets out a wail, and I return to the dining room to help.

Jenna's bouncing him and patting his back. "Maybe we should take him out. Sorry for the noise."

"I could take him for a car ride," Eli offers.

"Oh, but I want to see him," Mom says. "I wish I could hold him."

"Mom, I've got it," Jenna says tightly. She paces with him while everyone watches, but he doesn't calm down, even after he lets out a burp.

"We should go," Dad says.

"Not yet," Mom says with a quaver in her voice. "It's early."

Drew goes over to Jenna. "If you don't mind, I'd like to help. I haven't spent much time with my nephew."

Jenna's eyes widen. "Are you sure?"

"Gimme."

She hands Theo over. Drew tucks him upright against his

chest, letting Theo's head rest on his shoulder. "All right, little man, we're going to take a tour of the living room."

Within a few moments, Theo's wails quiet. We all go in the living room to see what Drew did.

He glances over at us, but keeps talking in a low voice to Theo as he walks a path around the perimeter of the room. Finally, he stops by the front window, still talking to the baby. Is he talking to him like a little adult?

"He's like the baby whisperer," Jenna says.

We all take a seat while Drew and Theo bond by the front window. Conversation is subdued because we're all straining to hear what Drew is saying.

A short while later, Theo is sound asleep on Drew's shoulder. He walks over to us. "Which room is his crib in?"

"How did you do that?" Jenna asks. "We can never get him to sleep without a car ride or a long walk. You just stood there."

A ghost of a smile crosses Drew's lips. "I told him a history of the events leading up to World War II."

"You bored him to sleep," Eli says with a laugh.

I laugh too. That's exactly what he did.

Drew shoots Eli a dark look. "I'll find the crib."

"It's in our room," Jenna says.

Drew takes Theo upstairs.

"I'm going to try that next time," I say. "I'll tell Theo all about the contract negotiations."

"I'll tell him about police procedure," Eli says.

"Here I was thinking I was doing a great job with the lullabies," Jenna says.

Drew comes downstairs. "You guys did good. Theo's great."

"Thank you," Jenna says.

"Yeah, bro," Eli says.

"You'd make a great dad," Mom says to Drew.

Drew exhales sharply. "Yeah, I already did that looking after my younger siblings after Mom passed."

"Dad worked a lot at the restaurant," Eli says. "But Caleb

was the youngest at eight. That's not the same as looking after really little kids or babies."

Drew mutters something under his breath, looking uncomfortable. Poor guy.

Mom turns to me. "And you'd make a great mom. You have great instincts and a lot of love to give."

"Not everyone needs to have a baby, Mom," I say before heading for the kitchen to clean up.

A moment later, Mom appears at my side. "I'm a little too gung ho about being a grandmother for the first time. I'm sorry if it sounds like I'm pressuring you."

I run the dishwasher. "It's okay." I start scrubbing the counters clean, waiting for her to leave. I'm a little stung that when we finally connect, all she seems to want is for me to be more like Jenna.

Mom sighs. "Are you happy? I just want you to be happy."

I look at her. "I'm trying to be happy. Honestly, it's a lot of work. I think I'm going to stop trying and just be whatever."

"That's very wise. I wish I had it together the way you do at your age."

I drop the sponge, stunned. "You think I have it together?"

"Absolutely. You made a life for yourself far from home, and you've made a success of your career in a very competitive industry."

My throat tightens. "Thanks."

She opens her arms to me and winces. She's still in pain from the surgery. I give her a gentle half hug.

When I pull back, she gazes lovingly into my eyes, and in that moment, I feel like I can trust her. "I'm in love with Dominic," I confide. "The single dad."

"Oh, honey. I'm so glad you've found love."

"Yes, but I can't figure out how we can have a future when we live on opposite sides of the country. It's stressing me out and making it hard to enjoy the time we do have together." *And he's tied to a daughter he doesn't want to share with me.* It shouldn't hurt as much as it does.

"You want my advice?"

I nod.

"Don't think so much. Just see what happens. I'm starting to see the value in making the most of every moment in the here and now."

I smile a little. "Now who's wise?"

"Learned the hard way."

"I'll try."

"Don't try. Just enjoy yourself. How often do you fall in love?"

Good question. I don't think I ever truly have before. Who knew my one-night stand could be my one true love?

I desperately want to believe in the happy ending.

17

Dominic

I answer the door at eleven a.m. on Sunday morning already smiling in anticipation of seeing Nora. Sundays are my visit days with her, though Lexi always stays with us too. I'm not sure if that's for Nora's comfort or her own. I'm getting used to it. She doesn't usually interfere, doing stuff on her phone, unless Nora goes to her specifically.

"Good morning," I say warmly.

Lexi looks made up today, hair perfectly styled in soft waves, makeup exaggerated on her eyes, and an outfit that looks less mom and more runway—a blazer with a gauzy scarf, tailored pants, and high-heeled boots. Nora is her usual cute self in a long purple tunic with floral purple leggings. Her hair is in pigtails.

"Hi, Daddy!" Nora says, throwing herself at my leg.

I cup the back of her head. "Hi, Nora."

Lexi flashes a quick smile, reaches behind her, and thrusts a booster seat into my hands. "Congratulations. Today is daddy-daughter day. I think she's used to you enough to visit without me. I'll be shopping in the city. I'll text you when I'm on my way back."

My stomach drops. "You're leaving?"

She laughs. "Relax. You got this. Bye, Nora. I'll see you tonight after dinner."

"Bye, Mommy!" Nora says, walking into my place and heading straight for PJ. She's never had a pet, and she's fascinated with him.

Lexi turns and hurries down the stairs.

"You could've given me a heads-up!" I call after her. "I could've prepared."

She doesn't bother turning around, waving over her shoulder. "You'll be fine. Have fun!"

I go back inside and quietly shut the door. Nora is crouching next to PJ, poking her finger in his nostril. He pulls his head back and gives me a beseeching look.

I join them and push her finger away. "PJ doesn't like it when you poke in his nose. Touch him like this." I take her hand and smooth it behind his pointy ears. "He also likes his chest rubbed." I show her that too. "Everywhere he can't reach with his own paws."

She copies me, rubbing his chest. "Okay."

I stare at her, wondering what to do with her all day. Lexi always plans the day, and I just go along. I don't have any toys for her here. Why didn't I get something? All I have are dog toys.

She pats PJ on top of the head. "Good dog, good dog." PJ lowers his head to the ground, giving her a resigned look.

At least she's potty trained. I don't even know how to change a diaper. I'm totally unprepared for this! Damn you, Lexi!

I stand and pace a bit, jittery with nerves. I could take her to the playground like we did yesterday. That lasted a couple of hours.

"Hey, Nora, would you like to go to the playground?"

She stands. "Hungry."

"Oh, you're hungry. Did you have breakfast?"

"Cheerios."

"Okay. But you're hungry again." I check the time on my phone. It's a little after eleven. Hopefully restaurants are open for lunch by now. I usually go grocery shopping on Sunday night, and I'm down to frozen burritos. Can you feed a toddler a burrito, or are the beans too hard to digest?

"What would you like to eat?" I ask.

She beams. "Moussaka."

I blink, surprised she knows that word. "I don't know where to get moussaka. How about pizza?"

She nods.

"Great! Pizza. And then we can go to the playground."

"Yay!"

I let out a breath of relief. This will all work out fine.

"Wa-a-h!" Nora cries, her half-chewed pizza showing in her open mouth.

Panic has my heart racing. The pizza lunch was supposed to be the easy part of the day. A bee landed on our table, and before I could stop her, she trapped it under her hand, and it stung her. I grab her palm and inspect it. The stinger is lodged deep.

I take a deep breath. "Okay, I need to take you home and use some tweezers to get the stinger out."

She wails even louder. "I want Mommy!"

"Mommy's not here. Daddy will take care of you."

"Mommy!"

I scoop her up, leaving behind the pizza. She eats so slowly, she only ate a tiny part of it in twenty minutes. I finished mine. I can always come back, right?

She writhes in my arms. "Mommy! Mommy! Mommy!"

People at the restaurant are staring.

I give them a reassuring nod. "Bee sting. I'm going to get her home. I'm her dad."

Most of them go back to their meals, except one older woman who continues to watch me as I take my sobbing daughter out to the car and wrestle her into the backseat. As soon as the seatbelt is in place, she stops fighting.

"I got a boo-boo," she says in a small voice, staring at her palm.

"I know. Don't touch it. I need to get the stinger out."

"Hurts," she cries.

I kiss her tearstained cheek. "I know. Just hang on."

I drive back to my place, my shoulders hitching up to my ears as I hear her pathetic little cries in the backseat. Every few minutes, she says, "I want Mommy."

I consider calling Lexi, but it would take her at least an hour and a half to get back here from the city. Nora won't cry for longer than that, will she?

By the time I get Nora into my place, now sniffling and crying alternately, my nerves are shot. And I haven't even done the tweezers part yet. Luckily, I'm used to dealing with animals in pain. This will be similar. I can do this.

I take her into the bathroom with me, find the tweezers, and sit her on top of the closed toilet seat. "Stay there and don't move."

She holds her hand up, staring at her palm. "Bad bee."

"Bees only sting if they feel trapped. Next time you see a bee, don't touch it, just let it fly on by."

"Bad bee."

"Okay, bad bee." I get some rubbing alcohol from the cabinet and disinfect the tweezers.

I kneel next to her. "I need you to keep very still so I don't hurt you."

Her lower lip quivers. "I want Mommy."

My heart clutches. *Kill me now.* "You'll see Mommy later. Daddy will take care of you."

"Daddy's in heaven."

I close my eyes for a moment. "Your other daddy, then." I grip her hand open and use the tweezers with my other hand. The moment I touch the stinger, she jerks.

"Owww! No, Daddy! No!"

I try to get a better grip on her arm, but she twists and slides out from under my grip, running out of the bathroom.

"Nora, wait!"

She runs to the front door and tries the knob. Luckily, she can't reach the deadbolt above it. When that fails, she dashes behind the sofa, squeezing herself in between the sofa and the wall.

There must be an easier way to do this. At work there's always a vet tech to hold an animal while I work on them. Sometimes we have to sedate them. Obviously, I can't sedate a two-year-old. What else do kids like? If only I had a lollipop to distract her. I pull my phone out, about to text Lexi, but pride holds me back. Ever since I learned about Nora, I've been pushing for more visits with her. If I can't handle my first unsupervised visit, how's that going to look?

Then I remember how good Eve is with her infant nephew. She always says Jenna calls her his second mom. She'll know what to do. I text her:

SOS. I have Nora all day by myself. She got stung by a bee, and now she's hiding from me after I unsuccessfully tried to get the stinger out.

I wait several excruciating minutes while keeping an eye on Nora. She's unusually quiet. I peek at her over the top of the sofa. She's standing very still, trying to hide.

I step away. "I wonder where Nora is."

She giggles.

Okay, I can rule out an anaphylactic reaction. I just need backup. My phone vibrates with a text:

Eve: *I thought you didn't want Nora to get to know me.*

Me: *This is an emergency. She's going to end up hating me if I have to keep chasing her to get the stinger out.*

Eve: *You're chasing her?*

Me: *She tried to run away. Now she's hiding. Please come over. I'll owe you.*

Eve: *I have no experience with two-year-olds. I'm sure you'll do just as well as I will.*

Me: *It's going terribly!*

I take a picture of Nora hiding behind the sofa and text it to Eve.

Eve: *Aww, poor thing.*

Me: *This is our first visit without her mom. If she's upset the whole time, she's not going to want to do it again.*

My eyes get hot. I swallow over a lump in my throat. I didn't think it would be this hard. I've been so careful to take things slow, letting Nora get to know me.

Me: *Please, Eve. I need you.*

The words are raw and naked and vulnerable. I clench my jaw, waiting for her response. Ever since Lexi, I lost faith that a good woman you could count on for the long haul existed, but in this moment, all I want is to count on Eve this one very important time.

Eve: *Heading over now.*

I close my eyes, relief washing over me.

And the moment I see Eve on my doorstep, smiling and holding a stuffed giraffe, it hits me—I need her not just for today but for always, a permanent part of my life.

"I brought a distraction," she says, wiggling the giraffe. "Theo won't mind sharing."

"Thank you," I manage.

"Where's Nora?" she asks loudly.

There's a rustling behind the sofa, but she stays hidden.

"Nora, my friend Eve came over to visit, and she brought something for you."

"It's my favorite stuffed animal," Eve says brightly. "A giraffe. Do you like giraffes?"

Silence.

Eve makes a shushing motion, handing me the giraffe, and then goes to PJ, where he's lounging in his bed. She picks him and the bed up, setting him down at the end of the sofa where Nora can see him.

"Since I can't find Nora, I'll let PJ play with my giraffe," she says, setting the giraffe against his side.

PJ slowly glances at it and then looks at her with his signature haughty look. Eve kneels next to him and pets him just the way he likes behind the ears while talking to him for Nora's benefit. "Isn't it a great giraffe? I knew you'd like him.

So soft and furry with just the right amount of neck to hang onto."

She stands and crosses to me. "It's too bad Nora's not here to see my giraffe."

I put my arm around her shoulders and pull her against my side, kissing her temple. "Thank you for coming over," I whisper near her ear. "I was losing it."

"You'll be fine. Did I mention I used to be a stubborn kid?"

"No."

"Oh, yeah. The queen of stubborn to my own detriment. I also ran away more than once. It requires patience, persistence, and—" she lowers her voice "—a little incentive." She winks.

I'm in love with you. My heart pounds, the blood thrumming through my veins. She's the woman I didn't believe existed. I want her with me for the long haul, a true partner in life.

Her eyes go soft, as if she heard my thoughts. It's probably written all over my face.

A shuffling noise draws our attention. Nora reaches over PJ to get the giraffe and trips on him. She lands sprawled on top of him, her injured palm hitting the giraffe. She wails at the same time that PJ yelps and leaps away, limping a little.

I go to Nora first, picking her up where she's sprawled across PJ's fleece bed. At least she had a soft landing. "Did you hurt your hand again?"

She nods, tears pouring down her face. "Bad dog."

Eve grabs the giraffe and makes it dance in front of Nora. "Say hello to Gizmo." At my surprised look, she lifts one shoulder in a shrug.

"Hi, Gizmo," Nora says in a weepy voice.

"Let's all go to the bathroom to get that stinger out," I say.

"How about we stay here on the sofa?" Eve says. "Nora can hold Gizmo. Would you like that?"

Nora nods.

Eve puts her on the sofa and hands her Gizmo. She turns to me. "Do you think she'd let me hold her?"

Nora babbles to Gizmo, touching her nose to the giraffe's nose.

I nod. "She'll probably be distracted enough not to mind. I'll go get the tweezers."

When I get back, Nora's sitting in Eve's lap, the two of them talking to the stuffed giraffe on Nora's lap. They look comfortable together already, both of them happy to be conversing with Gizmo. My mind skips ahead to Eve being part of Nora's life too. I like that idea. I'm not sure how it would work, but it feels right.

Eve looks up at me with a smile. "I've got my phone to shine a light on her hand."

"Great idea."

I sit next to them and pull Nora's hand toward mine. She snatches it back.

I keep my voice calm, even though I'm nervous about hurting her. "Nora, I need to get the stinger out, or it's going to keep hurting you."

"No."

"I have to."

"No."

Eve chimes in, "After you get the stinger out, we can go out for ice cream. Gizmo too."

Nora gives me her hand.

"Incentive," Eve says. She shines a light on Nora's palm with one hand and holds her wrist with the other.

I grip Nora's hand and slowly move in with the tweezers.

"Did you know today is Gizmo's birthday?" Eve asks. "Let's sing happy birthday to him."

Eve starts in an off-key voice, and Nora joins in. She jerks her hand a little as I work, but by the time they finish the song, I'm done.

"All better," I say.

Nora inspects her palm. "Band-Aid for my boo-boo."

"I can do that." I head to the bathroom, listening to the

happy sounds of my daughter and my new love, laughing and talking. This is the life I want for my future. Eve, me, Nora, and future children.

I shake my head at myself. I haven't even told Eve how I feel. For all I know, she could run straight back to LA. Of course, that's eventually where she'll end up. And I could never leave Summerdale, not with Nora here and my work.

What do you do when you finally see a fantastic future together, yet it's impossible?

18

Eve

"This may have been a mistake." I give Dominic a rueful look. We let Nora get a cup of chocolate ice cream, and she's wearing more of it than she ate.

We're at Shane's Scoops, the gourmet ice-cream shop in nearby Clover Park. I grew up next door in Eastman, so I know all the shops here. There's not a lot of people in the shop, probably since it's the last weekend of October and cold outside. There's just a couple of teenaged girls at one table, and an older couple at another.

Nora is still fishing out the melted soup of ice cream from the bottom of her cup. Ice cream runs down her chin and, even though I tried tucking a napkin into the top of her shirt, so much of it missed the napkin and went all over her light purple tunic. Dominic and I were so busy talking and eating our ice cream we didn't realize how messy she was until it was too late.

Dominic gets more napkins from the dispenser at our table and tries to clean her up while she ignores him and keeps digging into her cup.

"Pretty good, huh, Nora?" I ask.

"Yes." She holds the cup to her face and tries to lick the bottom.

"I think it's all gone."

She shows me the cup with a thin layer of melted ice cream at the bottom. "More."

"You can drink it. Like this." I hold up my own ice-cream cup and drink from the dregs at the bottom.

She does the same but angles it too sharply. Ice cream floods toward her face and fans down her cheeks and chin. She slams the cup on the table. "All gone."

Dominic grabs more napkins and dabs at her face.

"Did you bring a change of clothes for her?" I ask.

"I've got nothing."

She wiggles down from her seat and runs to the ice-cream case, slapping her ice-cream-covered hands on the glass and tiptoeing to look inside at all the flavors.

"Sorry!" Dominic says, pulling her hands away from the glass. He tries to clean the glass with the napkin, but it just smears it.

One of the two red-haired girls behind the counter walks around with Windex and a paper towel in hand. She's wearing a Shane's Scoops T-shirt. The girls have the same bright red hair as Shane O'Hare, the owner of the shop. I bet they're his daughters. They look about sixteen or seventeen and closely resemble each other.

"No problem. We're used to it." She cleans away the hand-prints. "You should take her to the bathroom and wash her up." She gestures toward the back.

Dominic takes Nora by the hand and walks with her to the bathroom. He may be able to get the ice cream off her face and hands, but her shirt is completely ruined. I don't see how we can take her to the toy store down the street when she's such a mess.

A red-haired man appears from the back of the shop. Shane. "How's it going today, girls?" he asks. He must be late forties by now, but he looks exactly as I remember him. When I was a kid and unbearably shy, he was so nice to me. He'd often give me free samples when I couldn't make up my mind without me needing to talk, only pointing at them.

"Fine, Dad," one girl says like she's super annoyed he asked how it was going.

"We told you we could handle the shop on a Sunday," the other says, parking a hand on her hip.

"Glad to see it," he says. "Don't forget to clean up the counters, tables, and the scoops before you lock up."

"We know," they drone together.

He cocks his head. "Abby, Hannah, have I ever told you how much I love annoying you?" He tickles one and puts the other in a headlock. They laugh and push at him.

I bite back a smile. It's so nice to see a happy family. My eye catches on Shane's Scoops T-shirts for sale on a small shelf to the side of the ice-cream case. They have kids' sizes. Perfect for Nora.

"Hi, can I get one of the Shane's Scoops T-shirts in a child size?"

Shane goes over to the shelf. "What size?"

"Oh, I don't know. She's two." I hold my hand out and lower it. "About this tall."

"Let's try this," he says, handing it to me.

I hold it up. "That looks about right. If it's a little long, that's okay."

He rings it up for me while his daughters whisper to each other behind his back.

"I don't know if you remember, but I used to come in here when I was a kid. Eve Larsen. I always loved this place."

He studies me. "Oh, yeah! I remember you with your dad. He always got butter pecan, and you would want to try samples before deciding. You're one of the few kids who would choose a different flavor every time you came in."

"That's right. Everything was so good I could never settle on just one."

"Why, thank you. That's good to hear since they're all made fresh in our shop. Do you live in town?"

"Just visiting. You have beautiful daughters."

His daughters blush as red as their hair. He smiles.

"Thank you. I've got two more at home, another daughter and a son."

"Do they all work for you?"

"Only Abby and Hannah are old enough, but their younger siblings are dying to get close to the ice cream."

The girls nod, looking proud that they get to work here.

Dominic appears with a clean Nora wearing a stained wet tunic. "This was the best I could do."

"I got her a T-shirt," I say. "C'mere, Nora. You get to wear this cool shirt with an ice-cream cone on it."

She runs over to me, and I show it to her. "Ooh!" She holds her arms up.

I guess I'm supposed to help her undress. I pull her tunic up and off. Then I grab some napkins and pat her chest dry before putting the new T-shirt over her head. Her arms get caught as she tries to push them upward while I'm trying to get them across to the armholes. After a few minutes of struggle, the shirt is on.

She looks down at it and rubs her hand over the ice-cream cone, smiling.

"Thank you," I say to Shane.

"Here." He hands me a plastic bag. "For the dirty shirt. You'll want to soak that with stain remover as soon as you get home."

"Thanks, we will."

"Congrats on your family, Eve," Shane says. "Hope to see you all back here again on your next visit."

My lips part in surprise. Do we look like a family? It never occurred to me that anyone would think I belonged with them like a real family unit.

"Thanks." My voice cracks.

Dominic holds the door open for me. And then Nora surprises me and takes my hand.

❧

It's only seven o'clock, and I'm exhausted. We took Nora to the toy store and got her a tricycle after she rode one at the store and loved it. We asked her if she had one at home, and she said no. Dominic said he's never seen her on one, so we bought the assembled one, took it home, and spent most of the afternoon walking with her along the sidewalk as she pedaled.

After that, we went to the lake to feed the ducks, had a little picnic dinner, and came back to Dominic's place. Dominic and I were so wiped out, we put a movie on his laptop for us all to watch. It's *Finding Nemo*. We're half asleep, PJ is snoring loudly as usual due to his squashed-in face, and Nora is staring with wide eyes.

"Should we have made her take a nap?" I whisper to Dominic.

"I don't know. Do two-year-olds nap?"

"I don't know."

"I don't think it would've worked. She's still raring to go."

The movie ends, and Dominic and I look at each other. We still have more than an hour before Lexi gets here.

"When's Nora's bedtime?" I ask.

"I don't know. Lexi didn't give me much to go on."

Nora climbs down from the sofa and starts spinning in circles next to the coffee table.

"Don't do that, you're going to get dizzy," Dominic says.

Nora stops and then starts spinning in the other direction. That's when I remember how Drew put Theo to sleep talking about boring adult things.

"Let's put on an animal documentary," I say. "It'll probably bore her to sleep."

"She likes animals."

"Okay, then, something else boring and age-appropriate."

Dominic finds a cooking show and puts it on. "Look, Nora, they're cooking up cool international recipes."

She climbs up on the sofa and squeezes between us. Within a few minutes, she's sucking her thumb and twirling her hair, her eyes blinking drowsily.

There we go. She'll be asleep soon. My head nods forward as I accidentally fall asleep and jerk back awake.

Nora climbs into my lap, curling on her side. I wrap my arms around her, loving the feel of her in my arms. I never knew what a special experience it was to hold a little one until I held Theo.

Nora reaches out and puts her hand on Dominic's arm, connecting us all together.

A few minutes later, Nora goes limp, asleep in my arms.

"She likes you," Dominic whispers.

"I like her too," I say.

He smiles at me, his eyes warm. "I'm so glad you came over today."

"So you're okay with me and Nora spending time together?"

"I am. I'd like her to know you."

I stroke her hair back from her face. The pigtails' hairbands fell out long ago. Her long dark hair is wispy and soft as silk. "I'd like that too."

I'm so relaxed with Nora cuddled against my chest and Dominic's warmth by my side. This is what it could be like, me as part of my own little family snuggled together on the sofa, our dog PJ snoring by our side.

A short while later, the doorbell rings.

"She's early," Dominic says, leaping from the sofa.

Nora's still sound asleep in my arms. I debate shifting her to the sofa, but hate to wake her in the middle of what could be an awkward scene.

Lexi steps inside. "I caught an earlier train." She freezes, staring at me holding her sleeping daughter. "What the hell is going on here?" she hisses.

"She fell asleep," I whisper, slowly rising from the sofa to transfer her to her mom's arms.

Lexi turns on Dominic. "The one time I let you have a solo visit and you have your latest lay take care of our daughter? This is the last time you get a solo visit."

"She's more than that," Dominic says.

"You said she was nothing special." Lexi takes Nora from my arms and heads for the door.

Nora lifts her head for a moment. "Mommy."

Lexi hurries to the door. "That's right. Your real mommy is here. We're going home."

The door slams shut behind her.

I stand there, numb all over and suddenly cold. I cross my arms, hugging myself. "I never wanted to get in the middle of your family."

He pulls me into his arms. "Lexi's just jealous. She'll get used to the idea of Nora meeting new people."

"This could cost you joint custody. She's very controlling."

"I'll talk to her."

I pull away, thinking about Lexi's lack of boundaries, her unannounced visits; even appearing early tonight was probably deliberate to catch Dominic unawares. "You need a lawyer." *Because I don't want to be the cause of you losing your daughter.*

"She just needs to cool off."

I give him a skeptical look.

"Besides, we don't know if…"

"If what?"

"If you'll be a permanent part of Nora's life. I get why Lexi's cautious."

"So now you're on her side. Before you said you'd like Nora to get to know me."

He runs a hand through his hair. "It's complicated. Can we come back to this when we know for sure if you're coming or going?"

"I'm going. It's just a question of when."

"We'll figure something out when the time comes. In the meantime, don't let Lexi ruin everything."

I sigh, weary to my bones. "You're right. Because then Lexi wins. I'd better go."

He kisses me. "I'll see you at the Halloween party."

"There's supposed to be an update on the strike at five

p.m. West Coast time on Halloween. The goal was to come to a consensus by the end of the month."

"And then we'll have that talk."

I hug him one last time before letting myself out.

One last party together, one big talk, two broken hearts. I want to believe it'll all work out, but I don't see how.

19

Dominic and I take one look at each other and crack up. I was afraid my dark mood would ruin tonight, but it's impossible to be miserable with the ridiculous look of his costume. He's dressed as Bleeker from the movie *Juno*, wearing sweatbands on his head and wrists, a T-shirt, gym shorts, and tube socks pulled all the way up. We're standing on Jenna's front porch, admiring each other under the porch light. I'm Juno, the pregnant teen.

He puts a hand to my fake pregnant belly. It's a pillow under my shirt. I added a hoodie to a tank top with a skirt and leggings under it. It was the best I could do for a costume at the last minute. *Juno*'s one of my favorite movies.

"How did this happen?" Dominic asks.

"'It all started with a chair,'" I say, quoting the movie. "How do you like me as a brunette?" I borrowed a brunette wig Jenna had from another costume.

He kisses me. "You look fantastic."

"Oh my God, you guys, I have to get pictures," Jenna says, peering over my shoulder at Dominic.

I step back to let Dominic inside for pictures. Jenna's wearing a bee antenna headband and has Theo in a bumble-bee costume that's like a big striped sleeping bag. He must be cozy because he's out cold. She's staying home for trick-or-treaters while Eli's out on patrol duty.

Mocha and Lucy circle us, sniffing. Dominic rubs the dogs' sides, one with each hand.

"You are so Juno and Bleeker," Jenna says, gesturing for where she wants us to stand. She sets Theo down in a portable crib next to the sofa and has us stand by the front door. "Dominic, I didn't think it was possible for you to look geeky, but the sweatbands do it." She laughs. "And the tube socks!"

"Thanks," Dominic says dryly.

He puts an arm around my shoulders, and I place a hand on my giant belly.

Jenna snaps a few pictures with her phone. "Mom would go nuts to see you like this."

I roll my eyes. "Don't give her any encouragement."

Jenna puts her phone in her pocket. "Have fun, you two. Theo and I are going to watch *It's the Great Pumpkin, Charlie Brown*. Now that I have a kid, I have the perfect excuse to watch all my kiddie favorites."

"I'm sure he'll love sleeping through it," I say. "Bye!"

The doorbell rings, and the dogs bark like crazy, rushing the door. Theo wakes with a startled cry. This is why I never ring the bell. Knocking or a key doesn't bother the dogs nearly this much.

"You've got trick or treaters," I say. "You want me to get it?"

Jenna scoops up Theo, rubbing his back as she heads for the door. "No, go have fun at the party."

I open the door to a group of three little girls dressed as a fairy, a ghost, and a witch.

"Trick or treat!" they chorus in unison.

"The lady behind me will help you out," I say, sidestepping around them. Dominic follows.

I glance over my shoulder at Jenna holding the baby cradled in one arm as she holds out the treats bowl to the girls with her other hand.

Before we reach Dominic's car, the girls are running to the next house, giggling. I wave to a group of parents standing in the street, who follow along with the girls.

"I miss trick-or-treating," Dominic says, opening my car door for me.

"The good old days. Now we have to buy our own candy and feel guilty for eating it."

He laughs and shuts the door.

It's only a five-minute drive to Wyatt and Sydney's house, not long enough for a deep conversation, but part of me wants to know if he smoothed things over with Lexi. I never want to be the reason he's cut off from his daughter.

"You're awfully quiet," Dominic says.

"Just thinking."

"About?"

"Did Lexi back off on her threat not to allow you solo visits with Nora?"

"I'm going to talk to her about it next Sunday during my scheduled visit. Trust me, Lexi needs time to cool off."

"I don't want to ruin things for you."

"You saved me last Sunday. When my little girl cries, it's like raw nerves everywhere. I was in a panic about what to do, terrified of screwing up. Then you show up calm as can be."

"I guess since she's not my kid, I don't have that raw-nerve feeling. I just thought about what might help her like I do with Theo."

"Maybe you should've been an ER doctor. You're good under pressure."

"I'm under pressure every week to make the show's deadline. It's script to shoot with a fast turnaround."

"Nerves of steel. Have you heard about the strike yet?"

I check my phone. It's seven p.m. New York time, which means only four in LA. "Not yet. I hope it's good news. Every day we're on strike loses the producers money, so they should want to end it."

"Not to mention the writers' lack of a paycheck. Are you doing okay?"

"Jenna covered my rent this month. I'm going to pay her back as soon as I can with interest."

"I'm sure you will."

We both get quiet, the lingering uncertainty about the future hanging between us like a big wall. One of us is going to have to scale that wall to get to the other. One of us will have to make a major sacrifice, and that can end badly with me resenting him or vice versa. If I wrote this, how would I craft a happy ending? Unfortunately, I'm known more for my cliffhangers than tying things up with a bow.

Maybe that means there is no happy ending. There's only the happiness I feel now. What do they say, better to have loved and lost than never to have loved at all? Fuck it, either way it sucks.

A few minutes later, Dominic drives up Wyatt and Sydney's long driveway to their house. It's a beautiful property with acres of woodland and rolling grassy hills. A large two-story house with gray clapboard siding is just ahead.

I point out the window. "Oh, Jenna told me about this. Look, a landlocked lighthouse." It's gray with a white top. Jenna says it's really a water tower, but the previous owner really liked lighthouses, so they made it look like one.

"So weird, right?" Dominic says. "I've been here before. Wyatt's been a big contributor to the animal shelter. We actually did a professional photo shoot here with guys and dogs for a calendar. They sold it around town."

"Now that you mention it, I remember Jenna saying something about that a while back. Shirtless guys and dogs. I need to see your month."

"Just mine?"

"Of course! I'm not going to ogle other guys. If the month just happens to flip through no fault of mine, I may get a peek though."

He laughs. "I'm sure she kept a copy. Eli was in it."

A few minutes later, we're at the front door. I'm normally

not into big parties, but I actually know a lot of these people through Jenna and Eli. Jenna's introduced me to her friends, and Eli's family all lives in town. Dominic presses the bell, and we hear dogs barking and stampeding toward the door.

"It's a real dog-friendly house," Dominic says.

A moment later, Wyatt Winters, a tall man with thick dark brown hair, answers, holding a white shih tzu wearing a pink bow in her hair. A pit bull mix wearing a ladybug costume, and a golden retriever wearing a tuxedo shirt stand by his side. "Snowball, Rexie, Scout, stand down," he commands the dogs, who instantly quiet.

He smiles widely at us. "Juno and Bleeker."

"Yes!" I say, pleased he knows the reference. "I thought I might have to explain us the whole night."

He steps back. "You're not the only one. My sister Kayla is Juno too." He turns, gesturing for us to follow. "Kayla, Adam! Come see this!"

I've met Kayla and Adam before. Adam is Eli's older brother. His wife, Kayla, is super bubbly and sweet.

We follow him down a hall to a large modern kitchen with granite countertops and stainless steel appliances. He gestures toward the counter where a variety of drinks sit along with plastic cups. "Help yourself. Beer's in the fridge." He sets the white dog down. I'm assuming that's Snowball. "Kayla!"

Kayla, a petite brunette, appears a moment later. Oh, wow, she really looks like Juno with her dark shoulder-length hair, big brown eyes, and petite size. "Eve, we're twins!"

I get closer, my eyes glued to her stomach. "It looks so real."

Kayla laughs and rubs her belly. "That's because it is. I'm eighteen weeks pregnant."

"Congratulations," I say. "Mine's just a pillow."

She pats my pillow. "I could tell. Still, a great costume. Oh, Dominic, you look good as Bleeker. Adam already took off his headband because he doesn't want to look geeky. I told him it was fun."

Adam appears a moment later, holding an open bottled water. He's tall and lean with muscle with short dark brown hair and a scruffy jaw. His brown eyes are a gentler version of his brother Drew's. He hands the bottled water to Kayla. "I told you the sweatband was making my forehead itch, that's all." He looks at Dominic, taking him in with a slow once-over of his entire costume. "Nice."

"I'm confident enough in my masculinity to dress like a geek," Dominic says.

"Maybe you're already a geek, so it's not hard for you," Adam says, elbowing him. "How're things going with Best Friends Care? It's all Drew can talk about."

"Really?" I say, surprised. Drew's pretty quiet when he works there. I couldn't even tell if he was enjoying himself.

"Oh, yeah. He talks about all the dogs and their different personalities, along with which ones might be good for therapy dogs."

Dominic cocks his head. "Huh. He hasn't said anything to me. Since I'm the one who chooses the dogs for the therapy program, I'd be interested in his opinion. Is he here?"

"He stays at the dojo on Halloween to give out candy to the kids. Besides, he'd never want to wear a costume."

Kayla wraps her arm around her husband's middle. "Drew's not much for parties, same as Adam here, but Adam endures for my sake."

Adam gazes at her adoringly, wrapping an arm around her shoulders. She smiles up at him before turning to us. "In two weeks, I'll have my ultrasound, and we're going to find out the sex and have a gender-reveal party. You're invited. It's going to be so much fun. I've got the decorations and a cake on order through Summerdale Sweets that will spill out blue or pink candy when you slice into it."

"Kayla makes everything a celebration," Adam says with a rare smile.

She nods enthusiastically. "I'm so excited, though I'm a little worried Tank will feel neglected."

"That's our dog," Adam says.

"He's very attached to me," Kayla says. "I plan on giving him a new toy at the party. It's a carrot that you hide treats in, and the dog has to work on getting them out. Our cat, Simba, will get some catnip."

"Sounds like you have the whole family covered," Dominic says.

Just then Sydney, Wyatt's wife, appears, holding baby Quinn on her hip. My heart squeezes at Quinn's chubby face peeking out through a teddy bear costume. Sydney's wearing bear ears on a headband.

"Adorable!" I proclaim. "How old is she now?"

"Nine months."

I rub the fuzzy brown bear costume on Quinn's arm. "Aren't you a cozy little bear?" I smile at Sydney. "And mama bear."

She takes in me and Dominic. "Love the cutesie couple costume just like Kayla and Adam."

"That's what I said," Wyatt says.

"Where's your bear ears, papa bear?" Sydney asks him.

He dutifully pulls them out of his back pocket and puts them on. He looks ridiculous, the ears too small for his masculine head. And the rest of him is in a beige Henley shirt and jeans. Not very bearish. Sydney's wearing a beige sweat-shirt with a bear on the front.

"Now who's the geek?" Adam quips.

He and Dominic snicker.

Wyatt bristles. "Just wait until the baby comes, and *you* have to wear family costumes," he says to Adam. "I'm sure Kayla will have many fantastic ideas for that scenario."

"Thank you, Wyatt," she says brightly. "I will. Let's all get a picture."

"I'll take it," I say. "You guys get together." I figure I don't really belong since I'm just visiting.

"You should be in it too," Kayla says. "Jenna's my sister-in-law, so that makes you my sister-in-law too."

The others gesture for me to join them.

"Okay, okay," I say with a laugh.

We all gather in close for a selfie.

"Next year we'll have to get Theo here with Paige and Spencer's baby Finn too," Sydney says. "We can do a baby group photo once they're all sitting up and fully immunized."

"By then, they'll probably be crawling," Wyatt says. "Quinn here's already on the go."

"It'll be like wrangling cats," Dominic says.

"What's your little girl doing tonight?" Sydney asks him.

"She went halfway around the lake trick-or-treating before it got dark," he says.

I bite my lower lip. I didn't even think to ask about Nora, and here I was, after just one day together, hoping I could be part of her life. I should've thought about her. Halloween is a big deal for kids, and I'm sure she understood what was going on. She'll be three in less than two months.

Sydney smiles. "What was she dressed as?"

He pulls out his phone to show her. "A princess. They had a little parade at her preschool."

Sydney and Kayla peer at the photo. "Aww!" they exclaim.

Dominic never shared that photo with me, even though I texted with him earlier today and saw him at Jenna's house. You'd think he'd share a pic. My throat tightens, and I push the hurt down. He starts to put his phone away.

"Can I see?" I ask.

He hands me his phone. My eyes sting. She's beautiful, of course. Her mom did her hair in ringlets with some glitter sprayed on it. I bet Nora loved this. She's wearing a rhinestone and ruby tiara, a necklace with a giant ruby, and a light blue satin and tulle dress. She looks so happy, beaming at the camera.

"Did you get to go to the parade, or did Lexi send you this?" I ask.

"I was able to be there in person," he says. "One of the many advantages of having Nora live here."

"That's great," I manage over the lump in my throat.

Dominic tucks his phone in his pocket, his gaze catching on mine curiously.

"Who wants a beer?" Wyatt asks, opening the refrigerator.

The guys amble over to claim their beers.

I focus on baby Quinn, telling myself Dominic didn't purposely leave me out of the Nora update. He probably rushed back to work afterward and forgot to mention it. Not like I even remembered to ask.

"Can you hold her for a minute?" Sydney asks me. "Bathroom break for mama bear."

I glance around and realize Kayla's wandered over to talk to another woman at the party.

"Sure," I say, a little surprised she asked me. I've never held Quinn before. I take her in my arms. Ooh, she's much heavier than Theo. "Hello, you," I say to her. "I'm Eve. I bet you can't wait to play with your cousin Theo. Give him a year or two to get interesting."

She stares at me with wide eyes and then puts a hand on my cheek. I smile, and she puts her other hand on my other cheek, so she's holding my face in her hands. Then she squeezes.

I pull her hand away and then the other. "Careful with my face. Let's see what interesting stuff you can play with." I get a red plastic cup and hand it to her. She flings it across the room. "Aren't you a strong girl? I see pitching in your future, or maybe football. Girls can play football. Girls can do anything they want. Don't let society or all that pink tell you otherwise."

The room goes quiet. Dominic, Adam, and Wyatt stare at me.

"What? It's never too early to teach them."

Wyatt shakes his head. "You sound just like Sydney. My daughter isn't going to play football. I'd have to wrap her in bubble wrap. I'm going to teach her everything I know about coding. Worked for me." Jenna told me Wyatt was a tech billionaire from a young age. He retired in his early thirties.

I lean my cheek against Quinn's soft cheek. "She can do both, though baseball might be safer, I agree with you there."

Quinn pats my head.

"See, she agrees!"

Dominic comes over to us, smiling at Quinn and chucking her under the chin. He turns to me. "You're a natural with kids."

"How come you didn't share about Nora?" I ask quietly. "I would've liked to see a picture of her in costume."

"I'm sorry. I didn't know you'd care about a preschool parade."

I shift Quinn in my arms so she can't pull my wig off. "I felt close to her after our visit. I'd like to know stuff if you still want me in her life."

"I do."

I swallow hard and focus on Quinn's sweet face. She's pushing at her bear hood. I pull it off for her and smooth her hair down. "Okay, I'd like that too."

"We should probably talk soon about—"

"I know. Not now, okay?"

Dominic

I never thought my one-night stand would turn into the best relationship of my life. It's almost too good to be true. Eve and I just work, and she understands about Nora, even wants to be involved with her. The only question is, how do we make the long distance work? Eventually she's going to go back to LA, and there's a lot of miles between us.

We're gathered in a basement theater room, watching *A Nightmare on Elm Street* with a few other horror fans. The smell of popcorn fills the air. Wyatt has one of those old-fashioned popcorn poppers on a cart in a kitchen area across the room.

"Want some popcorn?" I whisper to Eve.

She squeezes my arm. "Yes, please."

I go to get us a bowl and snag a box of peanut M&Ms from the counter too. Wyatt stocked this place well with movie popcorn and candy. A woman I don't recognize, not wearing a costume, operates the popcorn popper. Staff? I thank her and return to Eve.

I hold up the snacks. "Should we mix the candy in with the popcorn?"

"You have to ask? Of course! I used to drink my soda through a Twizzler straw too."

"Don't think it would be the same with your water. Besides, I didn't see any Twizzlers."

"Shh," a woman wearing horn-rimmed glasses and a tweed jacket says from the seat on Eve's other side.

"Sorry," I say. She's an older woman, maybe Wyatt's mom?

Eve and I dig into our popcorn and candy. I've seen this movie so many times I'm paying more attention to her than the screen. She looks so cute in the brunette wig. Her lips are shiny with butter, and it just makes me want to lick them and her neck and lower. It never seems to lessen, this want, no matter how many times we're together. Maybe we can leave after the movie and go back to my place. I don't get as much time alone with her as I'd like. Only on the weekends because she's adamant about being there for Jenna and Theo. I get it. They're family, and she came here for them.

She glances at me. "Good combo."

We are.

I nod and take some popcorn and candy together. I've been thinking about spending Thanksgiving with her. I took off work for the four-day weekend with an emergency service on call for my clients. I have some time off between Christmas and New Year's too. That will help with the long distance, but what about after that? Would she ever consider living here?

～

After the movie ends, the older woman stands and announces, "Intermission! Come back in fifteen minutes for the second movie."

I wander over to the kitchen area with Eve, and we set our empty bowl in the sink and throw out our napkins.

"You want to skip out?" I whisper near her ear. "We could go back to my place."

"You look so hot in those sweatbands," she teases. "How can I resist?"

Damn, I forgot I was dressed like Bleeker for a while there. "And you're the hottest pregnant woman I've ever seen."

"Why, thank you." She pulls her phone from her hoodie pocket. "Let me just check in with Jenna and see if she needs backup tonight."

I wait impatiently, even though I know Jenna's holding down the fort alone with the baby and a string of trick-or-treaters.

Eve stares at her phone, her eyebrows furrowed. "The strike's over."

My gut clenches. We both know this is goodbye.

20

———

"How soon do you go back?" I ask.

She slowly turns to me, looking a little shocked. "Back to work next Monday. We got everything we wanted. This is good."

"Great. I'm happy for you." I try to force some enthusiasm in my voice, but it sounds fake.

"Thanks," she says softly. "I knew I'd hear something tonight, but I guess I got distracted, and now here it is." She reads the screen again. "These are amazing terms, actually. I think they were losing a lot of money with the strike and didn't want to go through another strike again down the line. Wow. A win for the writers."

"We should probably talk."

"Let me check in with Jenna." She walks to another area of the basement for privacy near some workout equipment.

I shove my hands in my shorts pockets and then take them out, feeling ridiculous. I pull the sweatbands off my head and wrists and push my tube socks down to a normal level. I'm done with couples costumes. Playtime is over. Shit just got real.

I'm going to lose her. I feel it in my gut. I never thought I'd find someone like her, and now she's leaving. Probably for good.

She walks over to me, her expression closed. No bright smiles, no warmth in those blue eyes. "Jenna needs me. She didn't want to bother us at the party, but she's exhausted, and Theo's being fussy. Would you mind dropping me off there? You can come back to the party."

"No, it's fine. I'll drop you off and head home."

She heads upstairs. "Thanks for understanding," she says over her shoulder.

"Yup."

Eve goes to find Sydney to tell her we're leaving, and I guess she mentions that she's heading back to LA soon, too, because Sydney gives her a big hug. Eve waves to everyone else, and I wave from a distance, not in the mood to be social.

As soon as we're outside, I say, "I can visit you over Thanksgiving. It's only three weeks away. That's not too long to wait."

"I don't know. In the email, it said we should be prepared to do some writing at home over Thanksgiving break. I might only get one day off."

"Okay, okay. One day could work. We could do the turkey-and-fixings thing, watch football, whatever you want."

She stops me, putting a hand on my arm. "Dominic."

My stomach drops. I already know I don't want to hear anything after that. She's cutting me off.

"We'll figure something out," I blurt.

"I don't want you to fly cross-country just to spend one day with me. Don't you want to spend Thanksgiving with Nora?"

"Lexi's taking her to see her grandparents in Connecticut. She's hoping to reconcile with her sister."

"The one whose ex-husband she married?"

"He died, so she's hoping they can all move forward."

Eve shakes her head. "Real life is better than fiction sometimes."

I unlock my car, and she gets in before I can open the door for her. She doesn't want the couple gestures. She's pulling away. My gut does a slow roll. I get in on my side and carefully back out of the crowded driveway.

Once we're back on the main road, I say, "This can't be the end."

"We'll keep in touch, okay?"

"What does that mean?"

"I'll be back for Theo's first Christmas. I'll see you then."

"And then what?"

"Maybe we could see each other when the show's on hiatus. Because of the strike, it's later this year than usual. I'll be done by the end of January, and then we'll start up again for the next season in the spring. They already approved another season."

"So, what, we get February?"

"And maybe a couple of weeks into March. I know it's not ideal."

I drive in silence, mulling this over. The hard truth is, she doesn't sound like she has any intention of leaving LA. And I can't leave New York. Nora's here, and I want to be a big part of her life. I could always sell my business and start work in another place—though it wouldn't be easy—but I can't leave Nora. I already missed too much of her life. Lexi wouldn't want to move either. She loves being close to the city, and her family isn't far away.

By the time I pull up to Jenna's driveway, I have the sinking feeling that it's over. Still, I make one last-ditch effort. "I guess it wouldn't be fair to ask you to move to Summerdale permanently."

"I can only do my job in LA. It took me a long time to work my way up to steady work in a TV writers' room. It's a very collaborative process. We break the story together, come up with the arc for the season and each episode. And I'm in line for another promotion. Right now I'm story editor; next I could get a producer credit. I could move up to showrunner soon, in charge of the whole deal."

"And what if *Irreverent* gets cancelled?" I ask in the sick hope that will send her to me.

"I'll still be in a good position to pitch some of my own ideas for new shows that I run. Complete creative control. It's the top of the mountain for a TV writer."

"So leaving LA means you have to give up your career. You couldn't do it long distance?"

"Everyone else is there. They won't want me to phone it in."

I run a hand through my hair. "Why do I feel like I'm the only one upset that you're leaving? Don't you care at all? Ever since I met you, I've been the happiest I've ever been. I care about you. A lot. I never thought I'd feel this way about anyone again."

Her lower lip wobbles, and she bursts into tears. "I was trying to put on a brave face. I'm just going to be a complication for you and Nora, and long distance sucks, and I didn't want you to remember me like this, blubbering like a baby."

"Shh, you're not a complication. Lexi is, not you. Never you." I pull her into my arms and kiss her temple. "I don't want to lose you."

"I don't want to lose you either." She sniffles and pulls away, wiping her eyes. "I need to go in."

"Can I see you this weekend?"

She kisses my cheek, her tears wetting my face. "I think it's best if we say goodbye now." Her voice chokes. "I don't know why I said that stuff about my hiatus. Practically speaking, it won't work long-term, and I think we both know that." Tears stream down her face.

My vision blurs as I will my own tears back. "We don't know that for sure. We haven't tried."

"Bye, Dominic." She hurriedly opens the door and scrambles out of the car. I watch her fake-pregnant self dash to the front door, dying to snatch her back and kiss her to remind her what we have.

But I don't.

I sit there, devastated, watching until she goes inside.

"Bye," I say softly to the empty car. I want to howl, the pain tearing up my insides, my gut like acid.

The front curtain parts, and she looks out at me. I take off my seatbelt, about to go to her. She quickly shuts the curtain and turns away.

I let out a breath and jam my seatbelt back in the slot. I put the car in gear, back out, and hit the accelerator, tearing down the street, putting distance between us fast.

I slow down at the end of the block. Who am I kidding? You can't outrun this kind of pain.

Eve

Deep down, I always knew it would end. I just didn't know it would hurt this much. I loved, and I lost big time.

21

Dominic

Three excruciating weeks later, I'm about to leave work to fly to LA for Thanksgiving with Eve. She doesn't know I'm coming. Jenna gave me her address with a "go get her!" I'm not sure if Jenna's cheering for me and Eve to get back together, or for Eve to move to Summerdale permanently so the sisters can be reunited. Probably both.

I texted Eve regularly since she's been gone, and she's kept me up to date with her work, but she claimed she was too busy to talk on the phone. I can't win her back by text. Neither of us wants marriage after our terrible experiences, but I want to invite her to live together. Jenna said Eve's normal schedule usually gives her three months off a year. We could live together then. Maybe if *Irreverent* gets cancelled down the line, she could write movies from Summerdale. She writes feature films on the side already.

Is it wrong I'm hoping for her show to fail? Yes. But I don't know what else to do. All I know is that we belong together.

It's the day before Thanksgiving, and the office is closed and cleaned up. Drew is out back at the shelter behind the animal hospital, taking the shift I normally do.

I walk outside and make the short walk to the shelter, finding Drew in the dog area, refilling water dishes.

He turns to me. "All good here."

"Great. And Audrey's still good to share shifts with you for the weekend?"

"We got it covered, even on Thanksgiving. She's devoted to these cats. I think she'd take them all home with her if she could."

"Thanks. I really appreciate it. Any questions? Need anything from me before I go?"

"Actually, there is one thing." He walks over to a shelf and pulls a thick envelope off it.

"What's that?"

He hands it to me. "It's Audrey's book. Can you give it to Eve's agent when you're out there? Maybe they'll want to make it into a TV show or a movie. It's good. She let me read it."

I cock my head to the side. "I thought Audrey said it wasn't ready to send out. Every time someone mentions it, she says it needs another polish."

"She's just afraid of rejection. See if Eve's agent can help."

"I can't do this without Audrey's knowledge."

"I already sent it to all the literary agents and publishers I could find last week. This is the last piece of the puzzle. She'll be glad when I have good news to share with her."

I hand back the envelope. "Do you know nothing about women? Never go behind a woman's back. She'll kill you for this."

"She'll be relieved when she hears the good news." He thrusts the envelope toward me again, and I back up a step, refusing to take it. "I'll email it to you. Please just do this for her."

"Drew, seriously, you have to tell her what you've done."

"I will when I hear the good news."

"What if you don't hear good news?"

He goes back to the dog kennels. "I told you the book's good. She's going to be the next big thing, and she'll thank me in the end."

I think of sweet librarian Audrey, perpetually worried that

her book's not good enough yet. I haven't read it. Maybe Drew's right, and she just needs a push.

Or it could all blow up in his face. Just like my surprise visit to Eve. At least I have a semblance of a plan.

Or am I just fooling myself like Drew here?

~

Eve

I've got a supermarket Thanksgiving waiting for me in the refrigerator—rotisserie chicken, stuffing, and pumpkin pie. It's my reward for when I finish writing today. I got my own episode, and I plan to finish it over the long holiday weekend. I stare blankly at the blinking cursor on my laptop screen.

The problem is, I keep thinking about my life in Summerdale, and then the tears come, and I can't focus on work. I miss Dominic so much I ache. And I miss holding baby Theo, my weekly lunches with Mom, living with Jenna and Eli, family dinner. I miss little Nora with her big vocabulary and all the new friends I met. I even miss all my doggy friends—PJ with his haughty looks and the craziness of Mocha and Lucy. And the cool crisp fall days. LA is sunny all the time, no fall foliage on palm trees.

I sigh. My apartment seems so empty and quiet.

I'm lonely.

I drop my head in my hands, sadness weighing heavily on me. I've been going to bed early every night, and when I do, I dream of Dominic with his sparkling sky-blue eyes full of warmth and tenderness. And then I wake, and it hits me all over again. I lost the only man I've ever truly loved. A good man who was there for me when it counted.

I straighten and take a deep breath. Work is the only thing that keeps the tears at bay.

The doorbell rings. Strange. I didn't order anything. Maybe Jenna sent me something. She's good about sending flowers or candy gift boxes for special occasions.

I peek through the peephole and gasp. Adrenaline fires

through me. Dominic's standing there, holding a bouquet of red roses, a suitcase by his side.

I turn away, smoothing my hair down with shaky hands and patting my clothes, looking down at myself in a sweat-shirt and jeans. Oh my God, I can't believe he's here!

I open the door. "Dominic!" My knees wobble as I step back, the blood rushing to my head.

Strong arms wrap around me. "Are you okay?"

I hug him tight, pressing my cheek against his chest. "I'm just so surprised."

He cradles my face in his hands. "I missed you so much."

"I missed you too." I step back and gesture vaguely to my messy apartment. There's papers, storyboards, and Post-it notes scattered all over the living room and small dining area. "Sorry for the mess. I wasn't expecting anyone. I only have Thanksgiving food from the supermarket."

He brings his suitcase inside and returns to me. "All I care about is being with you." He hands me the roses, his eyes intent on mine, warm and tender. "Eve, I love you."

I stop breathing, every nerve standing on end. I want to tell him I feel the same, but what comes out is, "Oh."

"I should've told you before you left. And I'm not saying let's get married, but I'd like a future with you."

Hot tears prick my eyes, a rush of emotion making it hard to speak. Could I have a place with him and Nora? I want to believe in the happy ending.

"Eve?"

"I'd like that."

I set the roses on the coffee table and wrap my arms around his middle. He holds me close, stroking my hair.

I lift my head, meeting his eyes. "I love you too, but—"

"Let's stop at love. We'll figure the rest out."

I nod, even though my gut says it won't be that easy. And then he kisses me, and there's no need for words. Our bodies express all the love between us.

Dominic

Eve and I lie naked in bed on our sides, limbs entangled, relaxing in the aftermath of fantastic makeup sex. I stroke her hair back from her face, wishing we could always stay just like this, blissfully happy together, away from the outside world.

She sighs. "I know I want to stay together, but I'm not sure I can give up my career that was so hard won."

"We don't have to decide anything now. When you visit at Christmas, we'll work out some compromise that works for both of us."

"Don't you feel like that's just putting off the inevitable?"

"The inevitable is us being together."

She snuggles closer.

I change the subject, attempting to keep things light between us. "Yesterday, Drew tried to give me Audrey's book to pass on to your agent without her knowledge. And the worst part is, he already sent it to literary agents and publishers for her."

Her jaw gapes. "No!"

"Yes."

"That's awful. Behind her back! Should I tell Audrey?"

"The damage is already done. Drew has to confess and take the fall for that."

"You're right."

"I told him to tell her. I'll push him about it again when I get back."

She rolls out of bed. "Let me finish up this script today so I can take you around the area the next couple of days. When's your flight back?"

I prop up on an elbow. "Sunday morning."

"I can work more after your flight too."

"I'll just read quietly while you work. Can I read your movie scripts that haven't sold yet?"

She pulls her sweatshirt on, no bra. "As long as you promise not to pull a Drew and send them out without my knowledge."

I shoot her a dark look. "Believe me, I know better than that. She's going to be so pissed."

She looks around for her panties, and I find them on the nightstand, handing them to her. I admire her long legs as she gets dressed.

"He'll be lucky if she ever talks to him again," she says.

∾

"Okay, I'm emailing them to you now," Eve says from her spot at a round bistro table in the dining area. "Did you bring your laptop?"

"I did. Let me get that." I pull it from my small suitcase.

A few moments later, we're both settled with our laptops. I'm on the sofa; she's sitting at the table with headphones on.

I open the first script, titled *Once More With Feeling*. It's about sisters reunited. She mentioned to me before that she made this film with her own money and sent it to film festivals, but it didn't win. I like it. I can hear her voice in it just like she talks in real life.

She lifts one headphone away from her ear. "This is like our script club. I write them; you read them."

"First rule of script club is: you do not talk about script club."

She laughs. "*Fight Club*. Nice to see we have common movie references."

By the time I finish the script, my throat choked with emotion, I realize her talent. I can't ask her to give up her career for me. She needs to be here where all the TV and movie deals happen, where everything is filmed.

With a sinking feeling in my gut, I open the next script. Eve's still happily typing away over there.

By the time I finish the second script, I'm convinced she's going to be a huge success. I can't believe this hasn't been made into a movie yet. It's a twisty thriller set in a post-apocalyptic New York City.

She takes off her headphones and stretches. "Dinner break. Get ready to be wowed by my microwave skills."

I smile, my mind turning over how I can make this work. Hard decisions have to be made.

"You okay?" she asks.

"Yup. I'll set the table."

"Do you mind if we eat at the breakfast counter in here?" She gestures over to the bistro table covered in papers and scribbled notes. "I kinda have a system going over there."

"No problem. Eve, I've read two of your scripts so far. You're very talented."

"So's half this town. The other half should just go home. Ha!"

I find that hard to believe. I don't know if she's being modest, or if she truly believes she's just one of many. I could see the scenes unfolding like a movie as I read them. Not once was I bored, and I've never been a huge movie watcher. Or TV watcher for that matter. How ironic that when I finally fall in love again, it's with someone so different from me.

A short while later, we sit side by side on metal bar stools with our Thanksgiving dinners.

"Happy Thanksgiving," I say.

She holds up a drumstick, and I bump my drumstick against hers. "Happy Thanksgiving. Honestly, I'm in it for the pie. I'll probably finish it off for breakfast tomorrow."

We dig in to the food. Not bad for supermarket food. I normally go home to Michigan for Thanksgiving, and I'm a little spoiled with Mom's home cooking. Maybe next year I can bring Eve to a Russo family Thanksgiving in Michigan. Jumping ahead here. It's easier than figuring out the logistics of the here and now.

We finish dinner in companionable silence, both of us hungry. I didn't have anything to eat on the plane, slept a few hours in an airport hotel, and showed up here in the morning. Eve said she was too busy working to eat.

Once the pie is served, I say, "You know, Lexi always wants to go to the beach on vacation."

"Okay," she says slowly.

"Maybe she'd like it here. You're not too far from the beach. I could try to convince her to move here with Nora. You wouldn't have to give up your work, and I could find a job here."

"But you own your practice."

"I could sell it."

Her eyes widen. She eats some pie, looking thoughtful. Finally, she says, "Then I'm uprooting not one but three people."

"Let's put that as a possibility."

She nods, her eyes welling. "And another possibility is, I don't sign the contract for the next season in March and just work on my movie scripts in Summerdale. Of course, I could be broke."

I take both her hands in mine. "But you could live with me, so you don't have to worry about rent, and I'm sure you'll get more options or sales or whatever it's called. Eve, your scripts are amazing. These are the kind of movies I like to watch. Lots of high-stakes action with moments of humor. You even have one love plotline, where they both live at the end."

"I guess I didn't have much faith in love, though I tried."

"At least you had enough for one of your scripts. And what about finding work in the city? Aren't there some TV shows that film in New York that you could get involved with?"

"I don't have any contacts there. I'm not sure if my agent does either."

"There was a movie that filmed in Summerdale not long ago, through Claire Jordan's company. I remember everyone was excited about it. I bet we could get you some contacts through them. Harper Ellis was there, starring in it. Didn't Jenna grow up with her?"

She smiles. "That's right! I didn't realize Claire Jordan has her own production company."

We gaze into each other's eyes, the tension from earlier vanishing, replaced with hope.

"Claire Jordan works out of Connecticut," I say. "It must not be far from the city, which means it's commutable from Summerdale too."

"Cool. I'll look into it."

I take a bite of pie. Nowhere near as good as Mom's. I put my fork down while Eve continues to eat her pie with gusto. She probably never had homemade pie, growing up with her dad.

When she finishes her pie, she says, "I'll see if Jenna can get me in touch with Claire, and let my agent know. It depends if they have anything for me."

I shift toward her. "Are you saying what I think you're saying? You're seriously considering a future together in Summerdale?"

She fights back a smile and loses. "I'm seriously considering a future together. Location to be determined."

I kiss her all over her beautiful face. She laughs and throws her arms around my neck. The kiss turns carnal, lust igniting once more.

I scoop her up, cradled in my arms, and walk toward the bedroom.

"You're like the gift that keeps on giving," she says, smiling up at me.

"You're the best gift I've ever received. Now to unwrap you."

Eve

I'm back in Summerdale for Theo's first Christmas morning. The kid has no clue. He's sitting on Jenna's lap on the floor in front of the Christmas tree surrounded by presents. We're all sitting in a circle around him—my parents, me, and Eli—opening his presents for him and showing them to him one by one. Mom's doing really well, thank God. She's done her course of radiation, and the doctors are hopeful about her prognosis.

Just as we're finishing up the slow-present parade, there's a knock at the door. Dominic knows not to get the dogs worked up with the doorbell in case Theo's napping.

I pop up. "I'll get it." I hurry to the door and fling it open. "Merry Christmas!"

Dominic's standing there, holding Nora's hand. "Merry Christmas," Dominic says warmly.

"Merry Christmas," Nora says. "I'm three." She holds up three fingers.

I crouch down to her level. "I heard about that. That's awesome. Happy birthday."

"It was four days ago. You missed my party."

I glance up at Dominic, guilt twisting around my heart. I couldn't get here in time due to work.

"Next year," Dominic says.

I hug Nora and then hug Dominic even longer. Nora runs to the tree to see Theo's gifts.

There's a lot of noise as my parents meet Nora, exclaiming over her. Jenna and I have gifts for her. Eli hands them over.

Nora rips the wrapping paper to shreds and holds up a kiddie cookbook from Jenna and Eli, featuring her favorite cartoon princess. She tosses it to the side and opens my gift. Jenna looks to the ceiling.

"Ooh," Nora says. "A camera. I saw the commercial."

I help her hold it. "That's right. You just press the button right here." The camera is purple and made of some indestructible material.

"What do you say, Nora?" Dominic prompts.

"Thank you for the presents," Nora says.

Mom claps. "What nice manners!"

Nora gets right to work taking pictures of everyone. It's happy chaos as the adults exclaim over Nora and baby Theo.

"I'll get coffee for everyone," I say.

"We're going to need it to keep up with the little ones," Mom says happily.

I incline my head for Dominic to follow me to the kitchen. As soon as I get the coffeemaker going, I turn to him, prepared with my big speech.

He kisses me before I can get a word out. For a moment, I lose myself in it, wrapping my arms around his neck and melting against his body. The noise of my nearby family reminds me there's no privacy here.

I break the kiss, putting a hand on his chest. "Hold that thought. I've made a decision. I'm going to finish out my season on *Irreverent* and then go full-time with my feature-film writing. Maybe something will work out with Claire Jordan's company. Truth is, as much as I love writing for *Irreverent*, I've longed for more time to dedicate to my features. And even more than that, I've longed for you. I love you with all my heart."

He wraps his arms around me, whispering close to my ear, "I love you too, so damn much. I swear I'll do everything I can to support your dreams, and if that means you going back to LA for work here and there, I'm okay with that."

I pull back to look at him. "Really?"

"Really. I'm bringing another veterinarian into the practice. I'm making space in my life for you and for Nora and any future plans we have together."

I throw my arms around his neck and kiss him passionately. I never thought I could have this kind of love, the true forever kind. But it's here and it's real and it's everything.

"What's taking so long with the coffee?" Dad asks, interrupting the moment. "Oh. Sorry."

I glance over at the coffeemaker. It's full. How long were we kissing? "It's ready. Why don't you help me bring it to the living room?"

A few minutes later, we're all settled in the living room, sipping coffee and watching Nora try to teach Theo how to play with his baby toys. He's lying on his side watching her closely.

Eli pulls out his acoustic guitar and starts playing "I'll Be Home for Christmas."

Dominic entwines his fingers with mine. And as I look around that room in that golden moment, I know I made the right choice. I chose Summerdale for love and for family. For Nora, who needs her dad close.

And Theo.

And Jenna.

And Mom and Dad and Eli.

My whole life, I've longed for family. I've rediscovered mine, and one day maybe I'll have my own. It's a possibility I'm seriously considering.

After the song ends, Dominic says, "I have a present for Eve."

"Oh! I have one for you too. It's in my purse because it's fragile." I dash to the dining room to get it.

"Okay, I can wait," he says. My family laughs.

I hand him his present and watch him open the small heart frame. It's a picture of us in front of the Griffith Observatory in LA from when he visited me over Thanksgiving.

"Thank you," he says, kissing my cheek. "I love it. Why don't you sit on the sofa for your present?"

Eli gets off the sofa, gesturing for me to take his spot next to Jenna, who gives me an excited look before grabbing her phone and walking across the room. I glance around. "Does everyone know what my present is?"

Dominic opens a small velvet box, showing me a diamond engagement ring as he goes on one knee in front of me.

My hand flies to my mouth. I thought we both agreed marriage wasn't what we wanted after our terrible divorces. But then looking into his eyes so full of love, something gives inside me. The last little wall of defense crumbles.

He takes my hand. "It was only fear of making the same mistake again that put me off marriage, but with you, a forever commitment could never be a mistake. I love you, Eve. I swear I love you more every day, and if you agree to marry me, I'll love you for the rest of my life."

My lower lip wobbles, my throat too tight for words.

Nora rushes to his side and stares at me with big hopeful eyes. I blink back tears.

Dominic puts an arm around her. "Nora told me she's happy for you to be her stepmom."

"Is that true?" I ask her.

She nods. "I'm going to be the flower girl and throw petals down the aisle."

I smile at her through a blur of tears and turn to Dominic. "Yes!" I say with a choked voice. "I'll marry you."

He helps slide the ring on my shaky finger and crushes me in a hug. Everyone claps and cheers.

As soon as the noise dies down, Nora says, "I want a baby sister."

Dominic and I exchange a look. He perches on the arm of the sofa next to me. "What do you think about kids?"

I nod, tears spilling from my eyes. I never thought it would happen for me, never thought I could risk it, but after loving Theo so much and now Nora, I know I'd like a child of my own.

"Well, Nora, hopefully you will be a big sister," Dominic says.

"Make sure it's a girl," she says, shooting Theo a disgusted look. "Boys are boring."

I smother a laugh. "Boys can be nice too. Theo's a very sweet baby."

Nora crouches in front of him, where he's currently sucking his fist on a blanket on the floor. "Do you play dollies?"

He stares at her, looking startled.

"He doesn't even talk," Nora says.

"That's because he's still a baby," I say. "He needs to grow up a little first."

"Like me?"

"Yes, in two years he'll be lots of fun."

Nora throws her hands in the air. "Two years!"

Everyone laughs.

Dominic grabs her and tickles her. She giggles madly. "I'm

sure you'll love a new baby just like you love PJ." He pulls her in close, hugging her. "Sweet Nora."

"Just Nora," she says.

"That's right. Just Nora."

She flexes her muscles. "Strong Nora."

"Strong, smart, sweet Nora," Dominic says. He's such a good dad. I love that about him.

Jenna brings in a plate of Christmas cookies, and Nora races over to her.

Dominic takes my hand and gazes into my eyes. "I'm so happy. We can have a long engagement if you want. Just knowing we have a future together is enough."

My heart skips a beat. "Let's get married as soon as I'm back in Summerdale for good."

Eli goes back to playing Christmas carols on his guitar while Nora takes pictures in between bites of her snowman cookie, dashing from one person to the next. An overwhelming sense of peace comes over me. I gave up one path, and a bigger path opened for me, full of family and a true love of my own. Fantasies do come true. I should dream up more great stuff for my future. Because, now, I believe in a happy ending.

EPILOGUE

Two months later...

Dominic

Eve moved in with me in February. By Valentine's Day, we set a date for the wedding. It'll be this June. Now the week after Valentine's, we're hosting a housewarming party. Lexi and Nora stopped by earlier. Lexi is "evolving," as Eve says. After Lexi briefly dated a psychiatrist she met through work, who convinced her of the value of therapy and gave her a referral, she's been much easier to deal with. She apologized for not telling me about Nora, apologized to Eve for their rocky start, and worked out a custody agreement with me. Everything turned out better than I ever thought it could.

Eve and I made it an open house since my place isn't that big. People have been coming and going all night. Now it's just down to a small group: Jenna and Eli with Theo asleep in Eli's arms; Sydney, Wyatt, and baby Quinn, wide awake and crawling after poor PJ, who keeps running away. I bet when I adopted the old dog, he never expected to be dealing with tiny humans. It's good to keep him active.

Drew and Audrey are here too, though not together. Audrey's been taking turns holding the babies all night. You can tell she wants one of her own badly. She lights up when she holds them.

"I have an announcement," Sydney says. "I'm pregnant and—"

Everyone laughs. It's obvious she's pregnant, though she tried to keep it to herself in the early months.

"You didn't let me finish," she says, smiling widely. "It's twin boys. Identical."

Wyatt's chest puffs out. "Just shows how virile I am. Pow! My sperm split that egg in two."

"Whoa," Jenna says.

"Are you nervous about twins?" Audrey asks.

"At first I was in shock," Sydney says, rubbing a hand over her belly. "But then I thought how cool it would be. Twins have always fascinated me."

"We're getting help," Wyatt says.

"That too," Sydney says. "Wyatt's mom's moving in with us for the first year."

"You must be close with her," Eve says. She's a little nervous about meeting my parents when we visit them next week in Michigan.

"I am," Sydney says. "I lost my mom when I was twelve. Cynthia is like another mom to me."

Eve whispers in my ear, "I hope your parents like me."

I wrap an arm around her shoulders and give her a reassuring squeeze. "They'll love you."

She smiles and then turns to the group. "I have an announcement too. Claire Jordan wants to produce my script about an inheritance that has magical powers."

"I love that one!" Jenna says. "There's this kickass—"

I cut her off. "Don't give it away. We're supposed to keep it hush-hush until it's out. There's a twist ending that has to be preserved."

A chorus of congratulations follows until Sydney says, "Where's my congratulations?"

And then everyone congratulates her too, laughing, and making a big deal over her.

"In more good news," Audrey says, bouncing on the balls of her feet, "I finally got through my final polish, and I'm ready to send my book out to literary agents."

"Go, Aud!" Jenna says.

"Kick ass!" Sydney says.

"No," Drew says.

Audrey's brows crinkle in confusion. "No? But you haven't read the final version. It's much improved."

Drew looks queasy. "I don't know. I'm no book expert."

And then he leaves.

Eve and I exchange a look. I get the feeling Drew never told Audrey he sent out her book last November. Maybe he didn't hear back good news like he thought he would.

Audrey wrings her hands together. "Maybe I shouldn't send it out. Never mind. It needs another polish."

"Don't go by my brother," Sydney says. "He mostly reads nonfiction. He wouldn't know if your story was ready or not. If you think it's ready, send it out. You've waited long enough."

"Yeah, you're probably right," Audrey says, but she still looks uncertain.

Shortly after that, people leave, the parents looking tired and Audrey looking worried.

I shut the door and pull Eve into my arms. "Finally, I have you all to myself."

She gives me a sexy smile, running her hand over my chest. "What're you going to do with me?"

"Wicked, wicked things."

She pulls away. "Let me get PJ settled in his living room bed. We don't want him to see what an animal you can be."

"He'll want in on the action."

"Exactly."

I wait while she fusses over PJ just the way she cares for her nephew and my daughter and, one day I'm sure, our children.

"Okay," she says, heading for the bedroom. "Do your worst."

I grab her from behind, and she squeals. I gently bite down the side of her neck. She sighs and turns in my arms.

She gazes deep into my eyes. "My one-night stand became my one true love. I still can't believe that happened."

I cup her cheek. "That's because I was always your one true love."

"And my every night fling."

She pulls away and walks to the bedroom, stripping and flinging clothes behind her as she goes. The blood thrums through my veins, my breath accelerating. I strip in record time and pounce on her.

We fall into bed in a tangle of arms and legs, fueled by passion and love.

Don't miss Drew and Audrey's story, *Loving*, where the constantly circling pair may finally achieve coupling!

Audrey

I worshiped Drew Robinson as a kid. But then I grew up. That's my story, and I'm sticking to it.

He doesn't see me as anything but his little sister's best friend. He certainly didn't take me seriously when I shared from the heart. So humiliating.

Drew Robinson was the beginning and end of my belief in soul mates. I have to move on.

Drew

Soul mates. Forever love. *A fairy tale.*

Except now, with Audrey, I want to believe. I just hope it's not too late.

Sign up for my newsletter and never miss a new release! kyliegilmore.com/newsletter

ALSO BY KYLIE GILMORE

Unleashed Romance <<steamy romcoms with dogs!

Fetching (Book 1)

Dashing (Book 2)

Sporting (Book 3)

Toying (Book 4)

Blazing (Book 5)

Chasing (Book 6)

Daring (Book 7)

Leading (Book 8)

Racing (Book 9)

Loving (Book 10)

The Clover Park Series <<brothers who put family first!

The Opposite of Wild (Book 1)

Daisy Does It All (Book 2)

Bad Taste in Men (Book 3)

Kissing Santa (Book 4)

Restless Harmony (Book 5)

Not My Romeo (Book 6)

Rev Me Up (Book 7)

An Ambitious Engagement (Book 8)

Clutch Player (Book 9)

A Tempting Friendship (Book 10)

Clover Park Bride: Nico and Lily's Wedding

A Valentine's Day Gift (Book 11)

Maggie Meets Her Match (Book 12)

The Clover Park Charmers series <<sweet and sexy charmers!

Almost Over It (Book 1)

Almost Married (Book 2)

Almost Fate (Book 3)

Almost in Love (Book 4)

Almost Romance (Book 5)

Almost Hitched (Book 6)

Happy Endings Book Club Series <<the Campbell family and a romance book club collide!

Hidden Hollywood (Book 1)

Inviting Trouble (Book 2)

So Revealing (Book 3)

Formal Arrangement (Book 4)

Bad Boy Done Wrong (Book 5)

Mess With Me (Book 6)

Resisting Fate (Book 7)

Chance of Romance (Book 8)

Wicked Flirt (Book 9)

An Inconvenient Plan (Book 10)

A Happy Endings Wedding (Book 11)

The Rourkes Series <<swoonworthy princes and kickass princesses!

Royal Catch (Book 1)

Royal Hottie (Book 2)

Royal Darling (Book 3)

Royal Charmer (Book 4)

Royal Player (Book 5)

Royal Shark (Book 6)

Rogue Prince (Book 7)

Rogue Gentleman (Book 8)

**Check out my website for the most up-to-date list of my books:
kyliegilmore.com/books**

ABOUT THE AUTHOR

Kylie Gilmore is the *USA Today* bestselling author of over fifty humorous contemporary romances. Her series include Unleashed Romance, the Rourkes, the Happy Endings Book Club, Clover Park, and Clover Park Charmers. With more than three million downloads of her books, readers all over the world love escaping into her hilarious feel-good romances featuring strong bonds with family, friends, and community.

Kylie lives in New York with her family, a demanding cat, and a nutso dog. When she's not writing, reading hot romance, or dutifully taking notes at writing conferences, you can find her happily crafting what will surely be future family heirlooms.

Sign up for Kylie's Newsletter and get a FREE book! kyliegilmore.com/newsletter

For text alerts on Kylie's new releases, text KYLIE to the number (888) 707-3025. (US only)

For more fun stuff check out Kylie's website https://www.kyliegilmore.com.

Made in the USA
Las Vegas, NV
23 August 2022